Leopold

Leopold

THE LION'S DEN SERIES

DANIA VOSS

Edited by Kay Springsteen

Cover design by Christine Cover Design

Formatting by Eternal Daydreamer Publishing, Tori Alvarez

Visit Dania's website at:
www.daniavoss.com

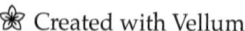 Created with Vellum

Rejected? Not *this* alpha

Returning home, newly divorced from the jerk her family warned her about, Brianna Palermo lands her dream job at The Lion's Den, a hot new nightclub chain that features live big cats, such as tigers, leopards, cougars, and lions. It's an amazing place to work, except Brianna is afraid of cats and does her best to avoid them. But less avoidable is her new boss, and owner of the club. He has kissable lips and a dominance she's drawn to. When he claims she's his, she promptly informs him she's sworn off relationships, and isn't willing to put her heart on the line again.

Leopold Van Housen has everything he could want – wealth, power, dashing good looks, adoring women in his bed, a precious black kitten, and most importantly - a lush, thick head of hair. When his positions as pride alpha and national shifter leader are threatened by the International Shifter Syndicate because he isn't mated and has no heir, he's infuriated. Things go from bad to worse when he meets his fated mate, and she rejects him, but then continues to work for him, teasing him with her tantalizing scent.

But Leopold isn't willing to give Brianna up without a fight, no matter how much her rejection stings. And threats be damned! His mother suggests he try a subtler approach to win over his delectable, feisty human mate. Easier said than done for someone who's used to his every command being followed without question.

The battle lines have been drawn. His reluctant little mate won't know what hit her and will be purring in no time. Let the wooing begin!

Contents

Chapter One

Leopold Van Housen did his best to shake off the feelings of dread as his driver led them out of Manhattan toward his family's compound in Claverack. His lion paced restlessly, sensing and bothered by Leopold's agitation. Normally comfortable in this Maybach, part of his and the Van Housen Enterprises Corporation's fleet, he was anything but. He tugged on his shirt collar that felt like a lasso around his neck and let out a sigh. How would he endure the over two-hour ride without clawing at the leather seats?

On the surface, the invitation to Sunday brunch wasn't all that extraordinary. He enjoyed the bountiful and delicious spread his mother's staff prepared every few weeks. No, what made this visit different was that it hadn't been a *request* to visit at all, so much as a not-so-subtle *insistence* that he did.

As the alpha of the first and oldest pride in the United States, Leopold didn't normally take kindly to subtle or not-so-subtle insistences – he made them and expected them heeded. Since the request came from his parents, he hadn't balked. Much. After all, who was he to pass up the bounty that awaited him at their ancestor's compound? A man, and lion, had to eat, didn't they? He hoped the debacle he'd be walking into wouldn't ruin his appetite.

Fuck. He didn't much care for surprises. He preferred everyone who dealt with him to be upfront and honest at all times.

At least it was a pleasant June morning. After brunch he could let his lion loose and roam the vast acreage his family owned. He could frolic in nature and play in the pond. His lion enjoyed a good frolic now and then.

The clicking of computer keys drew his attention away from his current concerns. His younger sister Chloe's fingers were gliding across her laptop keyboard in a flurry.

"Come on, it's Sunday morning. Dad has you working?" He'd been known to put in ungodly hours, but that came with the territory. Leopold was the top cat in the family's business enterprise in addition to his own businesses and investment pursuits. Chloe was a VP at Van Housen Bank, Corp. but from what he understood, she worked traditional banker's hours.

She slid him a playful sideways glance and a smile, her baby blues, similar to his own, sparkled brightly. "No, of course not. I'm not really working, just getting a handle on email. I get more unwanted email at the office than I do on my personal account."

He could relate. Spam email drove him crazy.

"It's mostly personal. As much as I adore your company, *Sire*, I wanted something to do during our drive up. I noticed you brought your laptop too."

His lion perked up at Chloe's deference. It was good to be king. The end of the year would mark ten years since he'd assumed the role from his father. He'd also be turning forty, not that anyone could tell by looking at him. His skin wasn't lined, his thick, blond mane was lush without a strand of gray, and he kept his body in optimal form. He was grateful for the shifter genes on the Van Housen side of the family.

He glanced at the laptop bag next to him and scoffed. Leopold doubted he could concentrate as they made their way to whatever impending disaster lie ahead in Claverack.

Chloe's brows drew together, and her smile turned into a frown. "What's wrong?"

"I'm not sure, but I have a bad feeling about today's visit at the compound." Leopold could have been creating a problem where one didn't exist, but his instincts told him otherwise.

Her eyes widened, and she rubbed her hands down her pretty flower-patterned summer dress. "Oh no. I haven't heard anything that would cause concern, but that doesn't mean anything." She wrung her hands over her laptop keyboard.

He should have kept his mouth shut instead of upsetting his sister. He couldn't help but confide in her. He adored her and trusted her implicitly.

"I'm sure it's nothing. My overactive mind getting the better of me," Leopold lied. He clasped Chloe's hands hoping to assure her everything was fine although he didn't believe it himself.

As a diversion for both their sakes, they discussed his plans for the expansion of his night-club chain The Lion's Den. A project near and dear to his heart. The chain featured what humans assumed were wild live big cats like tigers, leopards, cougars, and lions twice a week. In reality they were shifters – family, friends and family allies. They were featured for awareness and donation enticement for his actual wild feline sanctuaries and foundation both in the U.S. and Africa.

Currently The Lion's Den had several locations in the wealthiest zip codes in New York, with Albany being the first club location opened and the smallest. The Manhattan location had become his personal business and the chain's headquarters. He was looking to expand the clubs to the other states in which his sanctuaries were located and wanted to hire a General Manager to help make it happen.

They'd interviewed interested and qualified shifter and human candidates but hadn't found the right person yet. He was anxious to fill the position as quickly as possible, but not hastily.

Chloe beamed at him. Mission accomplished. It seemed he'd taken her mind off his concerns about today. "I'm so proud of this business venture of yours. In addition to the wonderful hot appetizers, high end liquor and a great dancing atmosphere, you're doing such great work bringing awareness to wildcat abuse and illegal hunting."

He appreciated her compliments but knew

there was more that needed to be done. This expansion would undoubtedly help.

When his driver pulled up to the compound the first thing he and Chloe noticed were more than the usual number of parked cars they'd expected.

"Looks like Mom invited some additional guests." Leopold wished he hadn't been right about today. *Shit.*

With shaky hands Chloe tossed her laptop into her carrying case and zipped it up, yanking clumsily on the zipper pull.

"It's going to be fine. Don't worry about a thing. I've got it under control." Leopold tried to assure his seemingly nervous sister.

They walked up to the main and largest home on the compound, built in the early eighteen hundreds, as if it were a death march.

"How can you say that? You don't even know what *it* is?" Chloe had a point, but he was the alpha, and it was his job to handle whatever came his way. And he excelled at his job if he did say so himself. His lion nodded in agreement.

As expected, they were let in by a member of his parents' household staff and directed to the expansive dining room.

Pausing at the entrance rather than stepping right in he noted his omega Oliver, a Siberian tiger shifter and his cousin, loading up his plate from the buffet. Not a good sign. Worse were the few members of the North American Shifter Collective for which he led the United States faction. Most worrisome were the members, all family, from the International Shifter Syndicate in the Netherlands and throughout Europe.

His lion growled. Leopold couldn't agree more. This brunch was a set up. For what, he wasn't sure, but he was about to find out.

"Shit." Chloe whispered.

He squeezed her hand for assurance. "It's going to be fine. Go fix yourself a plate." He squeezed again when she looked up at him with a doubtful expression.

"What are you waiting for," his asshole Uncle Hendrick said as he rushed past him and headed straight to the buffet line. His four-star army general uncle was in town? And in casualwear? Damn, now he *knew* this visit would become a shit show.

His stomach growled. He sighed and decided he may as well eat before the hammer fell. He acknowledged collective and family members alike while he filled his heirloom china with sliced turkey, prime rib, ham, and scrambled eggs.

He took his place at the head of one end of the

table. His uncle was seated at the other. His lion rolled his eyes. Leopold couldn't agree more. Hendrick's presence was almost enough to ruin his appetite, but not quite. Chloe was seated to his right and his parents to his left.

Leopold enjoyed his breakfast while half listening to the small talk taking place around him. He intentionally remained quiet, waiting for whatever was to go down. He wouldn't make it easy on his family.

His father was the first to speak to him directly. "Son, I'm sure by now you've surmised we have some important matters to discuss which is why we have a few additional guests for brunch."

No shit. He narrowed his eyes and glanced down the table to his uncle. Hendrick shrugged a shoulder and then shook his head. The general didn't know what the expanded family meeting was about? Interesting.

Chloe's eyes glistened with unshed tears. That did it. Enough with the cloak and dagger crap.

"Spit it out, Dad. What the hell?"

The pride's former alpha nodded. "Of course, alpha. As you know, at the end of the year you turn forty and it'll be ten years since you became alpha of this pride and assumed leadership positions with and within the North American Shifter Collective."

Leopold's lion stood tall and lifted his chin with great pride, his full, impressive mane a sight to behold. They were the shit, no denying that. "Obviously, a huge celebration is warranted. We didn't need a family meeting for that. Emails or group texts would have sufficed, don't you agree?" He doubted they were all here to discuss a birthday slash anniversary party, as appealing as the idea sounded.

His father cast his eyes downward, and his mother fidgeted in her chair. Hendrick, the asshole, smirked at his alpha. The elders and leaders around the table remained silent but all wore tense expressions on their cowardly faces.

Leopold slammed his fist on the table, causing the fine china to rattle. "Someone tell me right now what the fuck is going on or I'm leaving. Understood?" Anger spiraled from the pit of his stomach.

His mother reached over and gently placed her hand on his fist. It did little to comfort him.

"Senior leadership is concerned that you're getting older, you're not mated, and don't have an heir." His human mother almost seemed apologetic. As well she should, the cowardly men around the table leaving her to share this ridiculous and as far as he was concerned, inconsequential issue.

Too bad his lion hadn't gotten the memo and perked up at the mention of a mate and cubs. "Mating and heirs? *That's* what this meeting is all about?" He chuckled and popped a perfectly cooked piece of medium rare prime rib in his mouth. Scrumptious.

Finally, a male European elder from the Steenbock side of the family decided to speak up. "It's no laughing matter, Leopold. It's the future, the legacy of your pride, the collective *and* the syndicate. Don't let it all go to waste."

Leopold gritted his teeth so hard his jaw ached. He could hear the blood rushing through his head. "Are you fucking threatening me? If and when I mate and produce an heir is *my* business, *not* yours." His stomach clenched and he shoved his plate away. He couldn't believe this shit.

"I don't think anyone's making threats," Oliver said, seemingly trying to make peace.

"And *I* don't need to be handled right now, *omega*."

"Maybe you do, *Your Majesty*. Just hear senior leadership out for a minute." Oliver warned.

Leopold's lion could probably defeat Oliver's tiger, but he'd rather not put that theory to the test. His lion might ultimately be the victor in a battle against his omega, but he'd most likely walk away with a permanent limp and scars. Not a good look for him.

He leaned forward, elbows against the table and clasped his hands together. "Let's hear it."

"What's this Your Majesty business anyway?" a Baeten family elder asked.

Chloe sniffled. "That's because of me. I'm sorry. I started with the royal titles. Sort of as a loving sisterly joke. But it caught on among the pride. Leopold's an amazing alpha, leader, and businessman."

He winked at his sister. "My lion and I rather like the royal titles, thank you very much. You're making issue with *that*?"

His father waved a hand at the guests at the table. "Off topic. We are thinking of our collective legacy here, son. Even as shifters we don't live forever. We have to plan for the future. I groomed you for leadership long before it was yours."

"Mates don't just fall out of the sky. You all know that." Most met by accident. No one *demanded* a shifter to find their mate. It didn't work that way and everyone around the table knew that.

"We do, son. What's most important is an heir."

His mother's face lit up as if she'd thought of something spectacular to rectify this clusterfuck of a conversation. "What about Kaylee Hart? You've been spending quite a bit of time with her lately. And her parents are well respected in the pride even though they're managing a branch of the bank in Phoenix now."

He, Oliver, Hendrick, and Chloe groaned. His lion covered his eyes with his paws and shook his head. His mother seemed confused.

"Mom, Kaylee's not the one. She's – a diversion. She's slept with at least two other men at this table that I'm aware of, and Daniel and Benjamin." Benjamin was Leopold's beta, Daniel his delta. Kaylee was an opportunist. Producing an heir with her was out of the question. He had no intention of being linked to her for the rest of his life because of a child.

His mother's eyes widened in apparent surprise. Kaylee was also a kiss up to the former alpha and queen of the pride.

Oliver shivered and smiled at him. "Nah, Leopold is a catch. He has his pick of potential baby mammas. He's royalty in our circles. Hell, shave his head and he's got a Dr. Evil thing going although Prissy's black. A lot of women like bald men." His idiot omega laughed. Several around the table joined in. Assholes.

Shave his head? Never. His adorable little black kitten officially named *Priscilla* had been an unexpected rescue nearly six months earlier. The poor thing couldn't have been more than three weeks old and had been discarded like trash. Some people were so cruel when it came to black cats. Her eyes had been infected shut, she had been covered in fleas and starving. His lion had taken to her immediately, as his cub.

It had been touch and go in the beginning. He'd bottle fed her every two hours until she became strong. Her eye infections had cleared up to reveal the most beautiful deep blue color. She loved to cuddle, like he and his lion did. She was a good girl who he had trained to walk with a harness so he could keep her safe and was an honorary member of their pride, loved by all. And most telling, Prissy *hated* Kaylee. His kitten was an excellent judge of character.

Leopold was finished with the lot of them. "Laugh it up. I'm not going to be pressured into mating or producing an heir. By anyone. My life, my timeline. Is that it?" He was ready to head back home. He should have known better and stayed home.

When the elders turned their attention to his father Leopold's belly roiled with heat. Fuck.

"I'm sorry son, but if you're not mated by the

end of the year and at least making a legitimate attempt to conceive an heir, your leadership positions will be reconsidered and most likely reassigned. For our collective future."

Chloe gasped and Oliver cursed under his breath. So much for hearing senior leadership out.

Leopold's body tensed and his heart pounded against his ribs. He shoved at the dining room table as he stood, sending his Uncle Hendrick toppling over.

He was incredulous. Anger gnawed at him. "So, I lose my leadership positions as alpha, leader of the U.S. faction of the NASC, president of the NASC and can no longer oversee Van Housen Enterprises if I'm not mated and trying to knock said mate up? Have I got that right?"

Tears streamed down Chloe's face. He needed to get them the hell out of there.

His mother squeezed her eyes shut, seemingly fighting off her own tears.

"Not exactly," his father said, "You'd only lose your shifter related positions."

Fire burned in his veins. "You're kidding. You expect me to keep you all in your billions after you strip me of my shifter leadership? Why the fuck would I do that?"

"Don't be hasty, son. Think about it before you do something you'll regret."

Had his father lost his mind? Were shifters now able to get dementia?

"I've made our family tens of billions of dollars. My tireless work and Mensa level IQ got us securely to the number two spot on the Forbes billionaire's list. And what do I get for all that hard work while you've lined your pockets? Complete betrayal." Van Housen Enterprises Corporation was currently worth over one hundred and seventy-five billion dollars. Because of *him*.

"Cry us a river. You've done quite well for yourself. You're on the Forbes billionaire's list on your own," the Van Curen family elder spit out.

A thunderous roar escaped Leopold's lips. "I am allowed to have something for myself, aren't I? Not to mention the fact my clubs, foundation, hotels, and real estate interests employ family, pride, and collective members, so fuck off." He turned to his sister who was openly sobbing. "Get your things, we're leaving." She nodded sadly and left the room.

His weeping mother hugged him. "I'm so sorry. I had nothing to do with this decision."

He'd assumed as much. "Strip me of my shifter leadership in six months and I'll have no regrets walking away. From everything. From *all* of you."

Hendrick followed him and Chloe to the car. "I had no idea this was going down today. You have to believe me." Leopold may not have been fond of his uncle, but he sensed he wasn't lying.

Leopold allowed his sister a few moments to cry and collect her thoughts in the privacy of their car as they made their way back to Manhattan.

Chloe cleared her throat. "If they revoke your leadership, I'll quit the bank. We can start a new pride. A better one. I'll never betray you like the rest of the family has."

He pinched the bridge of his nose and growled. "There's no need for that. You've studied and worked hard for that position. Staying at the bank wouldn't be a betrayal. Regardless of what happens, you'll always be my sister."

She nodded sadly and sighed.

He needed his beta. Where the hell was Benjamin? He fired off a quick text to his second. Benjamin was at The Lion's Den HQ in Manhattan in the middle of an interview for the open General Manager position. That was unusual.

Two and a half hours later he and Chloe

stepped inside the club and Leopold was immediately struck by the most sinful, tantalizing scent. He drew in a deep breath and felt dizzy. His lion roared excitedly.

"Do you smell that?"

Chloe lifted her chin and sniffed. An easy smile spread across her face. "It's sweet."

"Not only that. It's my mate."

Chloe gasped, following him as he barreled toward Benjamin's office, bursting in without knocking. His mate's scent wrapped itself around him. His lion clawed at him to be released, but now wasn't the time. His mate was human and most likely didn't know shifters existed.

Threats to his leadership temporarily forgotten, he took in the sight of his queen. The gorgeous creature before him had luscious full lips, tempting curves encased in a sexy black pencil skirt and white silk blouse, glossy chestnut-colored locks, and soulful espresso brown eyes. Fate had been kind to him.

He stared at his mate, dumfounded, which was a foreign experience for him.

"Leopold, this is Brianna Palermo. Brianna, our fearless leader." Benjamin threw him a lifeline for which he was grateful.

She gracefully stood and extended her hand. Her eyes were slightly dilated, and she had a puzzled expression on her angelic face. Did she already feel the mating pull as he did?

His body zinged to life when their hands touched. He'd heard about this from mated pride members but hadn't believed. Until now. Her tiny hand trembled in his larger one. What he'd heard was indeed real.

"It's nice to meet you...Leo." His mate had sass. No one dared to sass him. Ever. He wasn't sure how he felt about that. Would he make an exception for his mate? He'd have to think about it. His lion nodded, whipped already.

"I'm Chloe, Leopold's sister. Why don't I show you around the club? That is if Benjamin doesn't mind." Thank god for his sister. Leopold needed to get his act together and act like the alpha and king his pride believed him to be.

"What the hell is wrong with you, dude? You've seen plenty of beautiful women before," Benjamin said after the ladies left his office.

Anger churned inside Leopold's chest. He grabbed Benjamin by the throat and squeezed. "Watch your mouth. Brianna's my mate."

"No shit," Benjamin squeaked out.

He let go of his beta and paced the room. "No shit. And wait until you hear what happened at brunch today. You won't fucking believe it."

Chapter Two

Brianna was impressed during Chloe's tour of The Lion's Den headquarters and club. They'd created a unique, exclusive experience for their patrons. Fortunately, the animal holding room had been empty. She shook her head. What had she been thinking applying for their General Manager position? She was deathly afraid of domesticated cats and thought working *here* was a good idea? The Lion's Den featured real live jungle cats on Tuesday and Thursday nights for Pete's sake, albeit for fundraising purposes, which she supported. She absentmindedly rubbed her scarred elbow.

She was led into a glorious executive furnished office. The beautiful cherry wood desk and bookcases, leather couch and chairs were a far cry from the dismal excuse of an office her ex-husband Grayson Reed had provided her to manage his small club chain Parlora, in California.

"May I?" Brianna asked Chloe, gesturing toward the desk.

Chloe's pretty blue eyes lit up and she nodded, then took a seat in one of the guest chairs in front of the desk.

Brianna settled herself behind the desk, sinking into the soft leather executive chair. She smiled at Chloe who watched her closely. She could definitely see herself working here every day. She reached into her purse for her stash of Hershey Kisses and grabbed two, offering one to Chloe. Silly, like little girls, they enjoyed their sweet treat in companionable silence until Brianna's phone rang. Her stomach clenched when Grayson's name appeared on the display. *Not now, jerk.*

Her body lit up inside, as it did when they shook hands, when Leopold strode into the office holding her resume in his large, strong hand. He made himself comfortable on the leather couch.

The unexpected attraction to her would-be boss should have sent her running, but she couldn't bring herself to do it. She was more than qualified for The Lion's Den General Manager position and she believed in the charitable work the club was associated with. Brianna would just have to deal with whatever attraction she thought she felt for the man because she had *no* intention of acting on it. Ever.

Brianna was finished with relationships. She'd crashed and burned so badly she wasn't sure she'd ever recover. Grayson had screwed her over good. Literally. She wouldn't allow herself to be vulnerable to a man again. Even someone as handsome and successful as Leopold Van Housen.

She stared at him, transfixed. The look in his ocean blue eyes was pure, hypnotizing seduction. If she got the job, Brianna hoped he didn't spend much time in his office, which was next door to this one. She'd have a hell of a time staying true to her resolve and keep her distance.

Mindful Chloe was observing them closely, Brianna turned away, breaking the spell, and reached into her purse for another sweet treat.

"Kiss?" What the hell was *wrong* with her?

Leopold's eyes widened and Chloe giggled. "If you're the one offering, of course."

The deep, sexy timbre of his voice sent need pulsing through her veins. Brianna needed to get herself together if she wanted to succeed at this job. Flirting with the owner was not a good idea.

She tossed him a silver wrapped chocolate and he caught it with a stealthy grace that made her breath hitch.

He smirked as he enjoyed the chocolatey treat with exaggerated appreciation, then licked his kissable lips. Brianna nearly moaned as her body hummed with awareness. Damn him. He obviously sensed what affect he had on her.

She needed to get things back on track. She was there about a job she wanted very much. "So, I assume Benjamin filled you in on my interview? As you can see from my resume, my education and experience are a great fit for this position. My only concern was if exposure to the animals was a requirement." She hoped Benjamin hadn't lied when he'd told her that portion of club operations was coordinated and managed through the LVH Feline Sanctuary, owned by Leopold himself.

Chloe turned to her brother; concern etched on her lovely face. Brianna's stomach clenched waiting for his reply. An animal exposure requirement was a deal breaker for her.

He raised a brow and grinned. "You don't like cats? And yet you applied for this job?"

It was a fair question. "I'm not fond of them, no. I applied because I know I can deliver on your vision for the club's expansion and in turn expand the work you're currently doing with the sanctuaries in the U.S. and Africa." She believed it in her heart, and she was excited to help him achieve his long-term goals and believed in what he was doing. From her perspective, it shouldn't require exposure to the animals themselves.

Chloe winked at Brianna, seemingly liking her response.

Leopold offered her a curt nod. "Thank you for your candor. And for your understanding and support of what I want to do. Exposure to the big cats isn't a requirement, but you never know. Over time you might find they're not so bad."

She doubted it but was relieved with his answer, nonetheless. "Maybe." When Grayson called her again, she turned her phone off. *Get lost, asshole. Don't ruin this opportunity for me.*

"You managed Parlora for quite some time. Are you tired of California?" His gaze was warm and steady, making her heart stutter.

She scoffed. "I'm the reason Parlora exists. My ex-husband's parents own Reed's Prime Steakhouse & Wine Bar on the West coast. He wanted to make a name for himself, independent of his parents." She'd made it happen and he'd taken all the credit. She was happy to finally be rid of the lazy, lying cheat.

Leopold grunted. "I'm familiar with that

chain. The Reed's seem decent and hard working. They've built up quite a name for themselves."

"Too bad their son is a lazy, entitled cheapskate," Brianna blurted out before she could stop herself. Obviously, her wounds were still raw. She'd have to take things one day at a time.

He nodded in understanding, seemingly not upset with her outburst. "I don't understand why Benjamin scheduled a Sunday morning interview. Did he inconvenience you? If he did, tell me immediately because - "

Brianna winced and felt her face heat. "No! I had to reschedule twice because my ex-husband kept stringing me along. Our divorce wasn't final until Friday and I hopped on the first flight out Saturday. I wasn't even able to make arrangements for an apartment. I'm staying at my father's house in Brooklyn. Bay Ridge. In my childhood bedroom." It was surely more than he or Chloe wanted to know. She couldn't help but feel like a loser. Thirty-five, divorced, unemployed, and living with her father. Her older brother Vito stayed in the finished attic. Keeping an eye on their seventy-one-year-old father.

"Oh no. I'm sorry things ended so badly for you. But maybe New York is where you were meant to be. Fresh start, new opportunities." She really liked Chloe. She was sweet, warm, and personable.

"That won't do at all. You should move in with me," Leopold said with conviction, as if they weren't complete strangers. And damn her traitorous body for shivering in delight at the thought of spending nights in his bed. She needed to get a grip.

"Look, Leo." Brianna began.

"It's Leopold."

His stuffiness amused her. He'd be so much fun to tease. "Right. I'm going to be straight with you because that's the only way I know how to be. I admit I'm attracted to you."

A wicked grin spread across his much too handsome face.

"*But* I am in no way looking to start up with someone new. Especially not my boss. Been there, done that. It was a disaster. I appreciate exposure to the animals not being a requirement, but if dating *you* is, which is illegal anyway, then as much as I don't want to, I'll have to withdraw myself from consideration for this job. I need you to respect my feelings about this or I'm not the one."

Leopold mumbled under his breath. "I would never ask anything illegal of you. Of course, I respect your feelings. I've never forced myself on a woman in my life. If it makes you feel protected, I can have Benjamin write a clause to that effect in your employment contract."

Brianna was disappointed and elated at the same time. "So, I have the job?"

His chuckle slid over her skin like a caress.

"Of course."

"Yay!" Chloe clapped and nearly bounced in her chair.

"Thank you, you won't regret it." Brianna vowed to get over her inconvenient attraction to her new boss and rock this new job. Chloe was right. This was the fresh start and amazing opportunity she needed.

"I know I won't. But do you honestly want to live with your father?"

She didn't, but felt she had no other choice at the moment. She couldn't, wouldn't move in with Leopold. Not if she knew what was good for her.

"There's a vacant three-bedroom condo unit next door to mine here in Manhattan. It's furnished. We let visiting relatives stay there. Leopold owns the building among many others in town."

The thought of not being under a microscope at her father's place while she healed her broken heart and regrouped from her disastrous marriage, held some appeal. Chloe as a next-door neighbor, even temporarily, was also appealing. It was a lot to ask, even though Chloe was offering.

"I don't know. I don't want to impose, and I'd pay rent. I'm no freeloader."

Leopold shook his head, a determined look in his eyes. "Absolutely not. It's an *intentional* vacant unit."

"Leopold's right. And this gives you the privacy you need right now. It'll help with the healing process after your divorce."

Chloe had a point. Brianna's head was still spinning. Time alone with her thoughts and to lick her emotional wounds was exactly what she needed.

"And you never know. Like with the big cats, you might find I'm not so bad after all," Leopold offered with a sly grin.

"Come on, Leo. We agreed. None of that." Brianna reminded him.

He sighed and nodded. "It's Leopold and yes, we did. I am a man of my word."

Why was she disappointed? Not getting involved with Leopold was the wisest course of action for her fragile heart. She'd be smart to remember that.

Shaking off her displeasure she tossed him another candy. "Right. Let's seal our deals with a kiss."

Leopold poured over the comprehensive background check that had been completed on his mate. It was considerably more thorough than what was usually conducted for shifter job applicants. Brianna had rushed out an hour ago, right after accepting his job offer and Chloe's temporary housing idea. Something about a twice a month Sunday dinner at her father's house. It would be her first since the divorce. His lion sulked in the corner of his mind, missing his mate already.

He wasn't the only one. Brianna's enticing scent lingered, making it impossible to focus on the intel in front of him. His ability to work with her next door beginning tomorrow would be next to impossible.

"You made arrangements to get her things moved to the condo after their dinner today?" Benjamin was seated in front of him reviewing paperwork for Brianna's first day tomorrow.

"Daniel's leading the team of deltas for her move. She said she didn't have much, mostly clothes. It was a brilliant move on Chloe's part to suggest that vacant unit. Brianna suggested she could move everything herself with her brother Vito's help. He lives at her dad's place."

Leopold grunted in disgust. He'd reviewed her divorce papers. She'd either had a shitty attorney or just wanted to be rid of her loser husband and didn't want anything even after so many years together. He tossed the pictures of Grayson Reed's many mistresses aside and shook his head. How could the man treat someone so precious so horribly? Brianna should have left his ass years before.

"Everything she did for this asshole, and he gets to walk away with just about everything? The monetary settlement wasn't nearly enough considering everything he'd put her through." Leopold scrubbed a hand along his jaw. They had family and allies in California. With one phone call he could put Grayson out of Brianna's misery for good.

"I'm with you on that. Grayson is a total douche. The complete opposite of his parents. I'm guessing by the time she was emotionally ready to leave him, she just wanted to cut her losses and move on as fast as she could. That's in the past now, alpha. She has *you*. And you'll treat her like the queen she is. Forever," Benjamin said, with sincerity in his eyes.

Brianna was his and the pride's queen, that much was certain. There was only one problem. "She doesn't want anything to do with me romantically. You added that clause to her employment contract, remember?" His lion whined at the prospect of never being able to mate his fated love.

Benjamin chuckled in his chair. "Well, yeah. Considering what she just went through, can you blame her? She's just trying to protect herself. And since she's human, she doesn't understand the mating pull or bond – yet."

"When did you become such an expert on women? Human or otherwise?" Benjamin played the field more than Leopold did. His obligations, both personal and for the family took much of his time.

Benjamin shrugged. "Chloe. She's a smart one."

Leopold grinned at the mention of his little sister. She was indeed a smart one. She'd saved his ass today and he wouldn't forget it.

"I don't know if you've heard, but everyone's wagering on whether you'll get Brianna to consent to be your mate by the end of the year so you won't have your leadership revoked." Benjamin informed him, wearing a cocky grin.

His pride were idiots. Betting on his future like that. "So? How do the odds look?"

"Most are betting you'll make it happen

before the deadline," Benjamin informed him with a self-satisfied smirk.

Leopold and his lion rolled their eyes. "Really? My beta and my best friend are betting *against* me?"

"Not exactly. I have no doubt she'll consent. Eventually. She's feisty and strong willed. I actually like that about her. I just think it'll take longer than the elders are giving you." Benjamin's expression sobered. "This leadership revocation threat is total bullshit. Hard to believe in this day and age."

"I couldn't agree more. The fucking nerve, especially after how wealthy I've made them all." Leopold could hardly believe it himself. But yet, there they were. Deadline looming ahead of him, and a mate who didn't want him. His own personal shit show. And he had front row seats.

"All joking aside though. So you know, there's a huge contingent of the pride that'll walk away if the shit goes down. We'll follow wherever you lead us, my liege."

Leopold blew out a frustrated breath. "Let's hope it doesn't come to that."

He scented a panicked Kaylee before she stormed into his office. Could his day get any worse? When Benjamin, the coward stood to leave, Leopold narrowed his eyes and growled at him. His beta promptly sat back down.

"So it's true? Your *so-called* mate got my General Manager position?" As usual, Kaylee's makeup was heavy handed, her jeans were so tight he didn't know how she could breathe in them, and she did something to push up the little bit of cleavage she had. Her dyed dark hair was a stark contrast to her fair complexion. The black leopard shifter had issues. It had been against his better judgement to sleep with her.

"Did you offer Kaylee the General Manager position before you interviewed my mate?" Leopold doubted it. Brianna was considerably more qualified by far. And he had no doubt she'd be more well liked than Kaylee would ever be. Kaylee managed one of his several New York The Lion's Den locations but had frequent personality clashes with employees and suppliers alike.

"Fuck no, I didn't. And if she says otherwise, she's a fucking liar," Benjamin said with fury in his eyes.

Her overly made-up face flushed. "No, he didn't. I just assumed -."

"That because I fucked you a few times you'd just be handed such a critical position?" Leopold snorted at the idea. No way in hell would he have entrusted Kaylee with the job. He considered it too important.

Kaylee Hart was not an emotional woman, but she managed to squeeze out a tear. "We're more than just fuck buddies. I...love you."

He and Benjamin barked out a laugh. "Like you loved Daniel? Or Oliver? Or Benjamin?" Leopold didn't have time for her theatrics.

"I think Hendrick too, if I'm not mistaken," Benjamin said. Leopold hadn't heard that. Damn, she had gotten around. Not that he cared. Kaylee was cat food compared to his mate.

She folded her arms across her small chest and narrowed her eyes. The *real* Kaylee before him now. "It's not like you said we were exclusive. I know you've been with plenty of other women – human *and* shifter, since we got together."

"True. That doesn't mean the job should be yours. It belongs to Brianna because she's the most qualified and that's final. She's your future queen and as such deserves nothing but your utmost respect."

Kaylee's mouth fell open and her eyes nearly bulged out of their sockets. "She doesn't even want you! You'll lose your leadership status before you can convince her to consent!"

Leopold waved a dismissive hand in Kaylee's

direction. "That's for me to worry about, not you. The pride will be fine regardless. If you feel that strongly about it, you're free to find another job and a different pride." He'd actually feel relieved not having her underfoot, especially now.

She threw her hands up and stomped her foot like a petulant child. "You should be nicer to me, *sire*. When your time starts running out, if you ask me nicely, I *might* save your ass and let you mate with me." She stormed out of his office much like she had stormed in.

Benjamin shook his head and cast his gaze downward. "Please tell me you won't mate with her, for fuck's sake, cousin."

"Never."

It was a bit after eleven that evening before Leopold was able to leave the office and head to the complex where his mate now lived. In lion form, he strolled down the hallway to her unit. He quickened his pace when he sensed her sadness and heard her muffled cries. He would have missed it were it not for his sensitive shifter hearing.

He passed Chloe's unit and planted himself outside Brianna's door. He'd promised Benjamin he wouldn't urinate all over the door, marking his territory, but rubbed his head against it instead. It would suffice.

His heart ached for the distress his mate was feeling, unsure of what to do to help her. Relief flooded him when Chloe opened her door and glanced his way with concern. His baby sister would know what to do.

Barefoot and in an oversized Maroon 5 T-shirt she hurried over and knelt beside him. She stroked his head with sisterly love. "It's okay, big brother. I promise." Chloe's voice was barely a whisper. Brianna most likely couldn't hear her.

How could it be? His mate was upset. It was his responsibility to ensure that never happened. Chloe hugged him around the neck, burying her face in his thick mane.

"I suggested she move here not only because she'd at least be living in one of *your* buildings, but because I knew she'd need some private time. To grieve the end of her marriage."

He didn't understand. Brianna's ex-husband was a piece of shit. She needn't waste her time or emotions on him. She belonged to *him*, even if she didn't know or understand it yet. Fate had deemed it to be so.

"Benjamin shared some of the awful high-lights of her background check with me. I know it's hard to understand why she'd be sad after leaving such an asshole, but my human friends have gone through the same thing. Even when they left jerks they didn't love anymore. It's all part of the process of moving on. Of healing."

He squeezed his eyes shut, shedding tears himself. He would be part of her healing and vowed to only bring his mate tears of joy.

Chapter Three

Brianna finished her ham and cheese omelet and took a sip of cranberry juice, enjoying the peace and quiet. Thankfully, the refrigerator had been stocked. Chloe had been so right, not staying at her father's house was the right decision. Although her father had said he understood her need for personal space the day before during Sunday dinner, she suspected she'd unintentionally hurt his feelings.

When Leopold's cousin Daniel had shown up at her father's place with five other Viking looking family members to move her meager belongings, she'd nearly laughed. She could have easily brought her things over in two trips in her Hyundai Kona. After her brother Vito, a former marine had given them all the third degree, she'd moved, temporarily, into the lavish *intentionally vacant,* furnished three-bedroom condo next door to Chloe.

After a much-needed cry and a relaxing soak afterwards in the huge master bathroom tub the night before, she was ready to begin the next phase of her life. Brianna looked forward to making Leopold's vision for The Lion's Den and the LVH Feline Sanctuary and Foundation a reality. It was a worthwhile cause and challenge she was ready to take on.

If she managed to keep her libido in check around her gorgeous new boss, she'd be golden. Nothing good would come from mixing business with pleasure. She'd learned her lesson with Grayson. She'd have plenty to keep her busy between her job responsibilities and reconnecting with her family and friends after a seventeen-year absence from New York.

Aside from the warm California weather, she'd only miss her in-laws. She loved Helen and Jonathan Reed. Helen had been like a second mother to Brianna, her own having passed away when she'd been ten years old. Her father had been left to raise her and her three older brothers with the help of the extended Palermo and Santoro families. Rosa Santoro-Palermo had been taken much too soon. Brianna missed her every day.

Helen and Jonathan had assured her they wanted to stay in touch after the divorce and her move back to New York. They'd written her flattering letters of recommendation. Were they feeling guilty about the circumstances surrounding the divorce? Possibly. They'd been furious at Grayson and had tried "talking sense into him," but in the end Brianna had been left with no choice but to leave.

Her own family had tried to warn her about Grayson early on, but she hadn't listened. Her embarrassment and feelings of failure were other reasons for her need for privacy. She wanted the space to regroup without being under a family microscope. She'd have to thank Chloe again for suggesting this temporary housing option.

Brianna deleted several unread texts from Grayson and grabbed her purse. *What the hell is wrong with you? It's over. Move on.*

She wouldn't allow him to ruin the first day of the rest of her life. The unexpected burly Viking dressed in a navy designer suit and tie with stunning green eyes on the other side of her door made her jump. "Can I help you?" She wanted to get to the office right away. She had a meeting scheduled with all the club managers and wanted to finish preparing.

"Good morning, ma'am. Leopold is waiting for you downstairs in the car." The brawny blond informed her.

"He is? Wait a minute. Who *are* you?" She assumed Leopold's driver, but why were they picking her up?

He nodded curtly. "Isaak Baeten." He gestured down the hall toward the elevator.

She proceeded down the hall to the elevator banks with Isaak Baeten two steps behind her.

"I'm Leopold's cousin. My brothers, Lars, Van, Espen, Finn, and I drive and serve as protection for family leadership."

So, this was how the ultra-wealthy lived. Brianna had done cursory research on the Van Housen family before deciding to apply for the General Manager position at The Lion's Den. Their extended family included the Baetens, Livingstons, Van Curens, and Steenbocks.

Their families were of Dutch descent from the Netherlands. The had originally migrated to a large area along the Hudson River in the present-day area of Albany, New York in the seventeenth century. The families played a critical role in the formation of the United States and had served as leaders in business, banking, politics, and society since migrating. The Van Housens were one of the wealthiest families in the world, currently number two on the Forbes list of billionaires.

The family owned much of Claverack, New York about thirty-five miles south of Albany. Their historical estate consisted of fourteen buildings including a massive main house and personal cottages.

Brianna hesitated before stepping out of the condo complex. Had she gotten in way over her head? The families were so far out of her league. Taking this job might have been a huge mistake. Her heart raced and she had an empty feeling in the pit of her stomach.

Unsure of herself, she glanced up at Leopold's green-eyed cousin, searching for something to calm her nerves.

Isaak gestured toward the revolving doors that led outside. "It's going to be fine quee... Brianna. There's nothing to worry about." His soft-spoken words and kind smile settled her nervous stomach a bit.

With renewed confidence for the day ahead, she took a deep breath and stepped out onto the sidewalk. It was just after nine and the city was bustling. Car horns were blaring, and pedestrians were quickly heading to their destinations on foot. Manhattan was open and ready for business. Brianna needed to be as well.

Her mouth fell open when Isaak pointed toward the running black Rolls-Royce limousine which appeared to be waiting on her. She raised a brow at him. "Really?"

Isaak merely shrugged. "The Phantom is part of the family's fleet." He opened the passenger door and rather than argue the point, she slipped inside.

Her ass, which had seen a few too many cannoli, sank into the most comfortable leather car seat – ever. Although Leopold was seated on the long seat, typing on his laptop, his presence filled the entire space of the six passenger ultra-stylish ride. His sandalwood scented cologne and personal musk swirled around her, making her tingle with unexpected desire. She shook her head and tried to focus.

"I could have driven myself, Leo. I'm quite capable, you know." She buckled herself in when the car pulled away from the curb.

"It's Leopold," he said, not looking away from his laptop.

"Right. I can drive myself in the morning."

"That won't be necessary. I'll have one of the Baeten brothers drive you every day unless you take your company car." His long, capable fingers flew over the keyboard with a precision she hadn't expected. Her body warmed as she watched him. *Get a grip*!

Had she heard him correctly? "What company car? Benjamin never mentioned anything about a company car. It's not necessary."

"An oversight on his part, along with your corporate credit card. Your Mercedes-Maybach GLS SUV and credit card are waiting for you at the office."

Brianna's muscles tensed and she saw red. "My little Hyundai Kona not fancy enough for the likes of a Van Housen?" For years Grayson had treated her less than because of her modest, blue-collar upbringing. She and Leopold may not be together, but she'd never tolerate being condescended to again.

Leopold sighed, turned his head, and focused on her. His steely blue gaze began a slow, sensuous stroll up her body, causing her to flush. She'd chosen a purple, short sleeved, mid-calf sheath dress with a short front slit for her first day. She felt pretty and professional dressed in her favorite color. The heat in Leopold's eyes suggested he approved. It shouldn't have mattered, but it pleased her.

"There is absolutely nothing wrong with your Kona. It gets great gas mileage and has an excellent safety rating," he replied in a calm, soothing tone. "Your position is important. You're the face of The Lion's Den now in addition to the visibility you'll have on behalf of LVH Feline Sanctuary and Foundation. You'll be hosting business meetings for the club and meet with wealthy foundation doners. They'll have certain expectations." Before she could object, he raised a hand. "I know it's not right and shouldn't matter. Sadly, that's the world we live in. I hope you can understand my perspective on this."

She hated to admit it, but he was right. Brianna hadn't considered she'd be representing the Van Housen family by accepting his job offer. Embarrassing them was the last thing she wanted to do. She'd suck it up and go along. They were silent during the remainder of the ride to the office.

The scent of lilies tickled her nose before she reached her office a few minutes later. She opened her office door to find it completely filled with vases and arrangements of lilies in every color imaginable. There had to be thousands – from white, and purple Asiatic to yellow sweet valley and bright red Corvara lilies.

Although no one had ever done something so spectacular for her before, from Leopold, it was highly inappropriate. They'd agreed. She navigated to her desk and read the card tucked in one of the many arrangements on her desk. *There is a place in my heart that has been waiting for you.* Secretly thrilled but equally annoyed at him, she glared at Leopold who stood in the office doorway, seemingly not bothered by the improper grand gesture.

"What the hell, Leo. How many lilies are in here?"

"It's Leopold. Only ten thousand."

"Whatever. *Only* ten thousand?" The man had more money than sense.

He shrugged and sniffed the beautiful standing arrangement of red twin Asiatics near the door. "Jay Z gave Beyoncé ten thousand roses a few years back. Consider it a welcome gift."

"They're married. And the card? Do you give *all* new female employees cards like that?" She planned on keeping it, regardless. That wasn't the point.

She shook her head, needing to prepare for her club manager meeting rather than argue with him. They'd have to convene in the conference room. Brianna grabbed her notes, company issued laptop, and left the room.

Two hours later, she was wrapping up a productive meeting with the five New York club managers and Benjamin. The blonds in the room, men and women including Benjamin were family members. Kaylee, the brunette who wore too much makeup and whose clothes were too tight – Brianna wasn't sure how she fit in with the group. She hadn't been very vocal during the meeting and had side-eyed Brianna a few times for no apparent reason.

They had all agreed, with a reluctant Kaylee, to review all current processes for areas to streamline and improve and to renegotiate purchase agreements from liquor to cleaning supplies. The goal was to create the most efficient operating model in New York before expanding across the country.

Everyone had welcomed Brianna again as they prepared to leave, except for Kaylee, who followed Brianna to her office after their meeting ended. She steeled herself for what she antici-pated was going to be some sort of standoff with the woman.

Kaylee took one look around Brianna's lily-filled office and shot daggers in her direction. "What the fuck is this?"

Could the woman be any more unprofes-sional? Her new position was going to be chal-lenging enough without having to deal with the likes of her.

"Never mind the flowers. Clearly you have a

problem with me. Why?" Kaylee and her shitty attitude wouldn't deter Brianna from her mission at The Lion's Den.

"For starters, the General Manager position was mine. Second, it doesn't matter that you might have Leopold's attention – at the moment. I've been loyal. He'll come running back to me so fast your head will spin."

Brianna assumed Leopold had his pick of eligible women to warm his bed. He and the family she'd met could grace magazine covers. Being confronted by his current lover who was also her employee didn't sit well. She'd expected more from him. That had been a mistake. Their flirting had to stop. Brianna would end up hurt in the end, and she'd been through enough. Never again.

"For starters, Benjamin and Leopold assured me I was their most qualified candidate. The job belongs to me. Second, you can have him. I'm no threat to you. The flowers were an overdone welcome to the company gesture. Nothing more." Brianna's nauseous stomach didn't agree.

Kaylee narrowed her eyes as if trying to decide if Brianna was telling the truth. "So, you're not together? You're not sleeping with him?"

Her stomach roiled. She knew she needed to

stay away and would, but why did the thought hurt so much? She barely knew the man. "You have to know this conversation is highly inappropriate. I'm not sleeping with the boss. It appears that's *your* job." Her patience had run thin.

Kaylee's lips twitched into a snarky grin; seemingly satisfied Brianna wasn't encroaching on her territory. The sooner she calmed down and left, the better.

"I'm going to need everyone's cooperation to make the club's expansion a success. I hope I'll have yours." Brianna wouldn't tolerate being undermined, even from Leopold's lover. If that's what he expected of her, then she wasn't the person for the job.

Kaylee hesitated a beat, nodded and left without a word. What had Brianna gotten herself into?

Leopold admired the Manhattan city skyline from the fiftieth floor of the Van Housen Bank, Corp. building. He'd dropped by to see Chloe after upsetting his mate with ten thousand lilies on her first day at The Lion's Den. He knew they were her favorite flower from the information in her background check. Perhaps seventy-five hundred wouldn't have angered her. He didn't know anymore. These were uncharted waters. Until Brianna, he'd never had to do much to get a woman's attention. He was the alpha, handsome, wealthy with a Mensa level IQ, and had a thick head of lush blond hair. He was a catch. Unfortunately, his mate hadn't gotten the memo. His lion whined in despair.

Chloe had been in meetings, unable to see him. When his father had heard Leopold was in the building, he'd asked to see him. Leopold had nearly refused, after the fiasco at brunch, but conceded to the former alpha out of respect. But his father was on thin ice with him. Leopold was still in charge and his father would be smart to remember that.

"The elders are thrilled you've found your mate," his father said after hanging up the phone.

Leopold's back was to him, with his hands in his pants pockets. "I don't give a fuck how the elders feel about it. I thought I'd made my feelings on their threat clear at brunch."

His father had the nerve to chuckle. "Oh, you did, son. It still doesn't mean their demands don't have merit."

That was debatable as far as he was concerned. "It doesn't really matter. My mate isn't interested in me romantically and hasn't consented to anything other than to work for me. She has no idea about shifters either so who knows what she'll do once she finds out." He felt helpless for the first time in his life and fucking hated it.

"It took your mother a little while to come around. I have no doubt Brianna will as well," his father said.

Leopold turned and faced his father in disbelief, his thoughts scrambling to understand. "What do you mean? She didn't adore you the moment you met?" Impossible.

His father belted out a hearty laugh. "Hell no. As a human, she hadn't known about shifters, nor did she understand the mating bond and pull. Obviously, she came around. Be patient."

Leopold scoffed. "The elders' threats and deadline don't really allow for much patience, do they?"

His father's face grew serious. "No. I'm sorry. They don't."

Leopold rubbed the ache on his chest. Something was wrong. He could sense it. His mate was upset. How could he know that?

His father glanced at him with concern. "What's wrong."

"I think something is wrong with Brianna."

His father smiled knowingly at him, momentarily making Leopold forget he was angry at him and the elders. "The mating bond is strengthening between you two."

Already? Even though his mate hadn't consented? He dialed Benjamin looking for answers.

"My liege," Benjamin said sarcastically.

Leopold had no time for jokes. "Is Brianna all right? How is her first day going?"

"As far as I know she's fine. I think her day went pretty well. Kaylee was - *Kaylee* at the manager's meeting, but everyone else was respectful and receptive to Brianna's approach to expand the club. She's been in her office all day."

Leopold disconnected the call. He needed to see his mate immediately and decide for himself that she was fine. He sensed her anxiety as he approached her office door a few minutes later. The scent of lilies had been drastically reduced as well. Had she thrown them all out? He didn't hear her crying and took that as a good sign.

He knocked twice and let himself in her office. All the lilies he'd given her were gone except for one vase of purple and yellow-tipped easy dance Asiatic lilies on her desk. He took that as a good sign too.

She looked up from her laptop and smiled, but it didn't reach her eyes. Her sadness hitting him in waves. Confronted with her anguish, his lion teared up, feeling as helpless as Leopold did.

"How was your day? Is everything all right?" He took a seat in a guest chair in front of her desk.

"It's great. I donated the flowers to local senior, homeless and women's shelters. I couldn't move around in here. I hope you understand." He could feel her unease. She was lying about doing great. Donating the flowers was a thoughtful gesture. His mate was a kind soul. His lion nodded.

"Of course. I'm sure they'll brighten up many people's day."

She handed him a sheet of paper. "I'd like to implement the Fallen Angel program at the clubs. I wasn't able to get it off the ground at Parlora even though I'd witnessed women in distress. I'm suggesting we hang up frames in the ladies' restrooms with the verbiage I just handed you and brief the servers, bartenders, and mixologists on the program."

The verbiage read –

Are you on a date that isn't going well?
Is your date not who they said they were in their profile?
Do you feel unsafe or even a bit weird?

Is someone bothering you or making you feel uncomfortable?

We're here to help, just go to the bar or ask your server for a Fallen Angel.

<u>Neat</u> – someone will escort you to your vehicle

<u>Dressed</u> – someone will call you a cab, Uber, or Lyft

<u>With Lime</u> – we will call the police

We will handle everything discreetly, and without a fuss. We want you to know that you are in a safe place and in good hands.

- The Lion's Den Management & Staff

Their female shifter patrons could most likely handle themselves, especially against a human man. But The Lion's Den attracted many human females. Brianna's proposed Fallen Angel program would provide another level of protection for the human women at their clubs, in addition to shifter security.

"Let's implement Fallen Angel right away. It's a great idea. Thank you for proposing it." His mate was amazing. How had he gotten so lucky? She'd make a superior queen of their pride. He hoped soon, regardless of this ridiculous elder deadline.

Brianna beamed at him, and his heart swelled. "I think the women who visit us will be grateful."

Leopold wanted to ask her to confide in him about what was bothering her, but Chloe burst into Brianna's office carrying two flutes of champagne before he could.

"Congratulations on your first day!" Chloe handed Brianna her champagne and to his surprise she drank it all in two huge gulps. "Quite a bit of family is downstairs on the dance floor eager to meet you. Come join us."

They were? Leopold discreetly inhaled deeply. Many of his female cousins and several of the males were in the building. He'd been too distracted by his mate to notice.

A sweet blush stained her cheeks. "They're here to meet *me*? Why?"

Because she was their future queen, that was why, he speculated. They were curious and nosey.

"They're excited you took the job and are helping Leopold expand the club. You're probably ready to unwind a little, right? Dance it out?" Chloe's enthusiasm was getting to Leopold, even though he didn't know what "dancing it out" meant.

He observed Brianna as her emotions played out on her beautiful face. She may have wanted to just head home and be alone, but she nodded and stood.

"Yeah. I like that idea a lot. Let's dance it out."

Ignoring him completely, the ladies both left her office without another word.

"Fuck me. I must be chopped liver." He found Benjamin in his office moments later wrapping up for the day. "The family *had* to come to the club on Brianna's first day?"

"Yeah well, I tried to convince them other-wise. To give Brianna some space before they all pounced. Sorry, man." Benjamin closed his laptop and stood. "We should go dance it out with everyone." Merriment danced in his cousin's eyes. He must have heard Chloe and Brianna.

"What the fuck does that even mean?" Leopold asked as he followed Benjamin out to the dance floor.

"Damn, Your Eminence. It's a *Grey's Anatomy* reference. You need to step up your game, or Chloe will end up as Brianna's person instead of *you*."

His lion growled at the thought. That most certainly wouldn't do. *He* was supposed to be his mate's *person*. Wasn't he? Leopold needed to binge watch some episodes and understand what the hell was going on. Step up his game as his beta had suggested.

Benjamin jumped into the throng of dancers. Many of them their relatives and pride members. The women had kicked off their shoes and most had a flute of champagne in their hand, including his mate. He'd need to keep an eye on her. A shifter's metabolism made it difficult to get drunk, unlike his human mate.

Brianna's smile was wide as she and his family danced to *Cupid Shuffle*. Heat burned low in his belly as he danced along, watching Brianna move to the right and then the left in the purple dress that hugged her sexy curves. His heart and cock ached with longing for his fated mate. His lion demanded to be set free and claim his forever. Sadly, they'd both have to wait.

After a few more up-tempo songs, where Leopold was able to show off his best moves, he had Brianna's undivided attention. She seemed to be feeling no pain after more champagne, while his relatives remained stone cold sober.

At his request, *Wobble* began playing. The dancefloor erupted in hoots and hollers. His body simmered with need watching Brianna shimmy and shake. Leopold gyrated his hips along to the song proving to his mate he could dance, hoping to make her curious about how he wielded the tool in his pants. Juvenile? Of course, but desperate times called for desperate measures.

When she wobbled in earnest from too much alcohol, Leopold decided to call it a night. His family had had their opportunity to meet and socialize with their future queen. She needed her rest.

"Let me get you home, Brianna. It's late." Leopold hoped she wouldn't put up a fight.

To his surprise, she wrapped her arms around his neck, her eyes dilated and dreamy. Her soft curves perfectly pressed up against him. His lion howled in excitement.

You're no fun, Leo." A wicked smile claimed her full, luscious lips.

"It's Leopold. On the contrary, I'm quite a bit of fun. You should give yourself a chance and find out." And oh, what fun he wanted to have with his mate.

After hugs and promises to get together again soon from his family and pride members, he drove his mate home in her company car. It wasn't a company car at all. The title was in her name, she just didn't know it. Only the best for his queen.

He'd gotten her home quickly. She'd kept her eyes closed and wore a sweet smile on her face during the short ride.

At her door she held her keys but turned and faced him instead of unlocking it. "I really liked spending time with your family. They made me feel so welcomed."

She shivered when he skimmed his fingers along the warm skin of her jaw. "That's because you're exactly where you belong, mate."

Her soulful eyes stared up at him innocently. Curiously. "What am I going to do about you, Leo?"

"It's Leopold."

Brianna's giggle was a mere whisper. "Right."

"How about this," he said before slamming his lips against hers for a hungry, passionate kiss. His pent-up desire for her since they'd met the day before guided him. He pressed her up against the door, ensuring she felt his engorged cock against her belly. The sexiest moan he'd ever heard escaped from her lips.

Nearing the limit of his control, his canines pierced through his gums. He ran them along the base of her neck where it met her shoulder. She shivered in apparent delight. How simple would it have been to mark and claim her right then and there?

Regretfully, Leopold backed away, placing much needed space between them. His lion growled in frustration. He was many things, but the last thing he would ever do was take away his mate's right to consent. Even with the elders' deadline and threats hanging over his head.

"Go on. You need to get some sleep," Leopold said, trying to regain his control and do right by his mate.

He'd never forget the hurtful expression on her lovely face after what she must have thought was his rejection of her. She nodded sadly, unlocked the door, and closed it softly behind her without uttering a word.

Chapter Four

Brianna re-read the card included with the vase of zebra lilies delivered to her a little while ago. *The only thing I want, is to be wanted by you.* As conflicted as she felt about it, she *did* want Leopold. She hadn't been able to quash the attraction regardless of what she told herself.

She'd enjoyed partying and dancing with his family and friends two weeks before on her first day at The Lion's Den. She'd been dancing it out with all of them until Leopold had joined their motley crew and driven her nearly insane with need. His dancing skills had made her curious of his skills in the bedroom.

So curious that when he'd dropped her off at her front door later that evening, she'd happily made out with him until he'd made her breathless from his ravenous kisses. She'd had a bit too much to drink but had intended on inviting him inside for more until he had appeared to change his mind about her, and suggested she got some rest.

His rejection still stung, but he may have done them both a favor by choosing to leave instead of pursuing more. Especially since she'd been drunk. She may have been disappointed by his change of heart, but she'd been impressed he hadn't tried to take advantage of her.

Then there was the issue of Kaylee. Leopold was in a relationship and shouldn't have kissed her in the first place. It had been the first time Brianna had knowingly made a move on someone else's man. What did that say about *her*? Even if that someone else was Kaylee.

Leopold had remained somewhat scarce since that fateful night. As much as she hated to admit it, she had missed seeing and speaking with him, but his absence had probably been for the best. Hell, the ink on her divorce papers was barely dry. Whatever Brianna *thought* she felt for him was better left alone and not acted upon.

Ready for her afternoon meeting with the club managers, she moved from her desk to her office conference table. Her managers filed in enthusiastically with a frowning Kaylee trailing behind them. *Heaven help me.*

"Welcome everyone. I know we're all busy so let's get started. Since we've re-negotiated our vendor contracts and achieved some significant savings from alcohol to cleaning supplies, I also want to adjust our sexy or naughtily-named drink specials."

Helen Reed had stayed true to her word and had assisted Brianna with all her vendor contract terms. The savings they'd negotiated would improve the club's bottom line and in turn add donation dollars to the feline sanctuaries and foundation. Brianna had been thrilled with their joint effort.

"I want to offer the sexy drinks every weekend at a slightly increased price with a foundation slash sanctuary donation tie in." All heads around the table nodded as she handed them the highlights of the plan. All heads except for Kaylee's.

"I'd like to incorporate a club loyalty program. Patrons enroll in monthly sanctuary donations. Depending on their donation amount, they'll receive discounts on food and drinks at the club, admission to the sanctuaries. As an additional incentive, they'll be invited to loyalty program, members-only events at the clubs and sanctuaries." She passed out the loyalty program plan, again to nodding employees, except for Kaylee.

Brianna wasn't deterred or discouraged. If Kaylee chose to be an unsupportive bitch, that was on her. As long as she stayed out of Brianna's way, they'd be fine.

"How has the Fallen Angel program been received?" Brianna hoped Grayson's reaction to the program in California had been wrong, and it had been well received at The Lion's Den clubs.

"It's been going well."

"Great feedback from the hume...women."

"We've had several ladies order Fallen Angels and we handled the situations discreetly just like our signs said we would, so I'd say it's been a success so far."

Benjamin acknowledged everyone around the table except for Kaylee. "I get the sense our female patrons feel a lot safer now when they come to The Lion's Den, thanks to this program. Thank you for implementing it. It was a great idea."

Kaylee rolled her eyes and scoffed.

Brianna had had enough. "Something on your mind, Kaylee? Let's hear it." She was so tired of her attitude. She didn't understand what Leopold saw in her.

Kaylee shrugged and glared at Brianna. "It's hard to take any of your ideas seriously, especially about the sanctuaries and foundation when you don't want to be near any of the animals. It's embarrassing. And talk about embarrassing, I never realized what ass kissers all of you are. Brianna's ideas aren't that great. Any of us could have come up with them."

Benjamin ground his teeth and held his hand up as if to say *enough!* Brianna couldn't agree more. "But none of us did, did we? Her ideas to realize Leopold's vision for the clubs and sanctuaries are right on point and you know it. She doesn't need to be around the animals to understand that cub petting operations, canned hunting, and animal abuse need to be abolished."

Before Brianna could stop them, all the managers around the table hurled insults and criticisms toward Kaylee. She allowed herself a minute to enjoy the moment. The bitch had it coming and then some.

"All right everyone, that's enough. I appreciate your support, I really do, but I'm capable of speaking up for myself."

Kaylee huffed like a petulant child.

"I assure you Leopold is fully on board with my plans. I've been given complete autonomy to execute this expansion project. You assured me two weeks ago that you supported the expansion plans, but if you're unhappy here, and the feedback I've received from some of the employees at your club indicates you're not, then you're free to find employment elsewhere." Not having to deal with Kaylee would make her job and life so much easier. Brianna doubted the woman would leave on her own accord though.

Kaylee raised a brow. "Are you firing me? You can't do that."

"You're pushing me in that direction. New York is an "at will" state. I can fire you with or without cause with no advance warning. I'd be careful if I were you."

Kaylee's laugh could only be described as evil. A shiver raced down Brianna's spine.

"Leopold would never allow you to fire me. I'd be careful if I were *you*." Kaylee's lips curled into a sinister grin.

Leopold admired his mate for maintaining her professional demeanor dealing with the likes of Kaylee. He'd heard enough from his office and felt compelled to join the shitshow that Kaylee had created. He chastised himself for ever getting involved with her in the first place. And to think his mother had suggested he mate with her in order to meet the elders' deadline. His lion's eyes widened in a panic. Deadline or not, he'd *never* agree to such a thing.

"On the contrary, I have no problem with Brianna firing you at all. I'm surprised she hasn't already if this is the way you've been conducting yourself since she arrived." Leopold hadn't wanted to undermine his mate, or he would have tossed Kaylee out on her sorry ass after the abysmal conversation he'd just overheard.

Kaylee gasped, and her cheeks turned a bright shade of pink. "Oh, alph. Umm."

Everyone in Brianna's office, except for his mate, smirked in his direction.

"Did you, or did you not tell Brianna you would support her plans for the club's expansion?" He doubted Brianna lied about what Kaylee had said to her two weeks ago.

Kaylee wrung her hands and her gaze darted to Brianna before turning back to him. "I…"

"Let me make this perfectly clear in case you're unsure. Brianna is acting on my behalf on all matters regarding the club's expansion and donation integration with the feline sanctuaries and foundation. She has my full support in *all* matters. If you're not on board and can't contribute meaningfully and professionally to our plans, then hand in your resignation by the end of the day. Go to Phoenix. I'm sure your parents would be glad to see you. I won't tolerate another minute of your attitude or bullshit. Am I understood?"

Kaylee's eyes glistened with unshed tears. It may have been an act, but he didn't give a shit. She was threatening his plans and future with his mate, and that was unacceptable.

She nodded and wiped her eyes with the back of her hand. "Of course. You both have my full support. I'm sorry." Although she sounded sincere, Leopold was skeptical. Time would tell and if she fucked up again, she'd be sorry.

Brianna rewarded him with a warm and inviting smile. He felt her gratitude deep in his soul. She'd had the situation well in hand before he'd stepped in, but he'd wanted to demonstrate he had her back.

"I hope I wasn't interrupting, that wasn't my intention," he said, anxious for her meeting to end. He had plans for their afternoon.

As if on cue, everyone at the conference table gathered their things, preparing to leave.

"Of course not. We were just about finished. I'll email everyone updates on our plans. Thank you all. What did you need?" Brianna's gaze lingered over him, then she lowered her eyes. She was lovely in her form fitting navy and flowered print dress. Professional yet feminine. His lion moaned in appreciation. Indeed, fate had been kind to Leopold in regard to his mate.

"Wonderful, there's someone who dropped by a little bit ago that I wanted you to meet."

She squealed when international action film star, heartthrob, and his cousin Dirk Van Curen stepped into her office. Kaylee had the good sense to excuse herself and leave without so much as a glance in Leopold's direction, while the rest of his family greeted Dirk with hugs and claps on the back.

They'd hadn't seen Mr. Hollywood in nearly a year. He'd just wrapped up filming his next highly anticipated action-adventure flick and had been on location in France, Spain, Portugal, and Morocco.

Poor Brianna stood there with her mouth hanging open and her eyes wide, after his family had left and only she, Dirk, and he remained. The spell broke when her cell phone rang. She hurried to her desk and connected the call.

"I told you to stop calling me. Get over yourself and move on." She whisper-shouted into the phone before disconnecting the call.

Dirk raised a brow and turned to Leopold. "It's the asshole ex-husband," he told his cousin.

"I'm so sorry about that. I— I— I'm so sorry. I'm not sure what to say." Brianna's face was flushed, and her breathing seemed rushed.

Leopold clenched his teeth. His mate was starstruck over his cousin. Jealousy, naked and cruel, gnawed at his insides and he hated it.

Dirk clapped him on the shoulder. "Give her a break," he whispered. "I know to *you* and everyone else, I'm just family, but to *her*, I'm this larger-than-life celebrity. Don't forget why you asked me here today."

Leopold nodded, reminding himself that Brianna was *his* mate, not Dirk's. It was natural for her to be a bit awestruck. He couldn't very well blame her, Dirk was a huge star, but that didn't mean Leopold had to like it.

Dirk extended a hand and went to Brianna. "I'm Leopold's cousin, Dirk Van Curen. It's a pleasure to meet you. I've heard so many wonderful things about you."

Brianna trembled so much as they shook hands, Leopold was afraid she might pass out. "You're Leo's cousin?" She glanced at Leopold curiously as if she didn't believe Dirk.

"I'm afraid it's true. We used to take baths together when we were little boys." Her sweet giggle was Leopold's reward. God, she was adorable.

"Leo splashed around way too much for me." Dirk commented.

"It's Leopold." He reminded his cousin.

Ignoring him completely, Dirk picked up his mate's cell phone. "Want a selfie of us for your social media?"

Her smile lit up her face. "You don't mind? I don't want to impose. I'm sure you and Leo have plans. I don't want to keep you."

"Don't be silly. I'd be happy to."

Leopold kept his emotions in check while his cousin cozied up to his mate for their multiple selfies. She seemed happy and that was all that mattered to him. Dirk graciously signed several sheets of club letterhead for her to give to her family. Her bright smile reached her eyes and for that he'd always be grateful to Dirk.

She shook Dirk's hand again, appearing calmer and more collected. "Thank you. You've been so nice. I won't hold you up. You and Leo can…"

"I'm here to take you to lunch, unless Mr. Boss Man is working you ragged." Dirk turned back to him and shrugged. Idiot.

"Really? You want *me* to join you for lunch? What do you say, Mr. Boss Man?" She directed her amused gaze at him, and Leopold's heart did a little flip. He was going to beat the shit out of his cousin when they were alone and mar up his pretty face.

He rolled his eyes. "Mr. Boss Man would never run you ragged. How does *Tutti i Fiori* at my Manhattan LVH Luxe Hotel sound?" Leopold had already reserved a small private room for the three of them with several standing arrangements of multi-colored lilies, hoping he hadn't overdone it so he wouldn't upset her.

Brianna's appreciative grin pleased him and his lion. *Eat my dust, Dirk. Mr. Boss Man rocks and don't you ever forget it.*

Dirk extended his arm and his mate happily accepted it. Leopold sighed and shook his head as he followed behind the two of them on the way to the elevator. He hoped he wouldn't regret asking Dirk for his help.

"Hey everyone! I'm in Manhattan on my way to lunch with my gal pal, and General Manager of The Lion's Den clubs, the beautiful Brianna Palermo," Dirk said to his cell phone camera, hamming it up for his social media followers in the back of their car on the way to his hotel for lunch. Brianna was all smiles as she waved to the camera.

Leopold clamped his lips together and swallowed his laughter watching his cousin's silly antics, but his heart turned over in his chest seeing his mate happy and enjoying herself. It was his job to ensure she'd always be happy after all. He'd do whatever it took.

Dirk put on a pair of dark aviator sunglasses and a club logoed baseball cap before they all exited the car at the hotel a few minutes later. *Interesting accessories with a designer suit.* He didn't envy his cousin in that regard. Out of a concern for privacy, he'd been careful not to disclose where they were having lunch in his video.

His hotel concierge swiftly and discreetly guided them to the freight elevator, familiar with the drill whenever Dirk was in town. In moments they were led to their private room without incident. It was bright and airy with an amazing view of the city. The round table normally sat ten but had been set with three chairs for them. Dirk tossed his sunglasses and cap aside and sighed, seemingly relieved he hadn't been recognized.

Brianna glanced around the room, taking it all in. She sniffed the colorful lily blooms in one of the several standing arrangements and nodded. "Thanks for not overdoing it, but flowers weren't necessary. I have that vase of lilies on my desk at the office, remember?"

Leopold shrugged. He'd always ensure she had fresh lilies from now on. He held out the center chair for her and she eagerly sat down. He and his cousin took their places beside her.

Dirk eyed him curiously. "What did you overdo?"

His mate explained before Leopold could. "On my first day at The Lion's Den, he got me ten thousand lilies. They completely overtook my office! I had to relocate my manager meeting to the conference room."

Dirk shrugged, apparently not understanding the issue, just as Leopold had expected. "Didn't Jay Z give Beyoncé ten thousand roses a few years back?"

"See?" Leopold said.

His mate shook her head and sighed. "They are *married*. Leo and I aren't and will never be a couple." She busied herself by reviewing the menu. He'd called ahead and had requested a sampling of the most popular items *Tutti i Fiori* offered.

He could admit her rejection stung, even though he knew it was only temporary. His lion whined at the tone of her declaration. Especially after the fevered kisses they'd shared two weeks ago. He longed for a repeat performance – and more.

Leopold felt and appreciated his cousin's sympathy. "Never is a long time. I know he can be a pain in the ass sometimes, but you could do a lot worse than Mr. Boss Man."

If *that* was Dirk's idea of talking him up, Leopold was in big trouble. His lion covered his eyes with his paws and shook his head.

"I have done worse. *Much* worse. That's why I don't want to pursue a relationship with *anyone*. Especially Mr. Boss Man. Been there, done that. Have the divorce papers as a souvenir." She looked up from her menu, with what appeared to be a forced smile. "Who's hungry?" She was right, it was time to change the subject. He didn't want to upset her.

A male server and pride member wheeled a cart into the room with their first courses. "How does steak tartare toasted baguettes and lobster bisque sound to start with?" Brianna was served first, a genuine smile on her face now. She nodded.

Dirk crunched down a steak covered baguette with gusto. "Sounds good, but what else did our fearless leader request for us?"

Brianna hadn't picked up on Dirk's alpha reference and enjoyed her appetizers, none the wiser.

"Your lunch also includes veal filled ravioli in a creamy mushroom sauce, lobster risotto, roasted duck breast, three of the prime tomahawk steaks with merlot sauce, parmesan roasted fingerling potatoes, and bacon wrapped asparagus – for sharing. And strawberry-lemon cake with vanilla gelato for dessert."

Brianna nearly choked on a spoonful of soup. "Oh, my gosh. That's a lot of food for the three of us, don't you think, Leo?"

The server raised a brow but remained silent.

"I don't know about my cousin, but I'm starved. Bring it on. If we have anything left, we can always take it to go." Like himself, Dirk was a lion shifter with a huge appetite. Leopold doubted there would be much left over, if anything.

His mate chuckled, and his heart turned over. Damn he had it bad for his human mate. If only she could allow herself to be guided by their instinctual bond.

"Our family has had nothing but wonderful things to say about you. It seems like I missed out on a great time at the club on your first day." Dirk glanced at him with a smirk on his lips.

Her eyes widened, as if surprised. "Really? They have? You did miss a fun time actually. Everyone was so welcoming. It almost made me feel like part of the family. I absolutely adore Chloe. I'm temporarily living next door to her."

Until she moved in with *him*, he mused. The sooner the better, his lion in full agreement.

"They're excited about your plans to help Mr. Boss Man expand the clubs and increase awareness and donations for the feline sanctuaries and foundation. I'd like to help. Just let me know what you need and consider it done." Dirk sliced into perfectly prepared steak and groaned in appreciation after he'd popped it in his mouth.

Leopold acknowledged his cousin's generous offer while he loaded his plate with the mouthwatering lunch items he'd selected for them. He was grateful for his supportive family, excluding the asshole elders.

His mate took tiny bites of her meal compared to the lions at the table. It was endearing.

"How would you feel about lending your name to a high visibility charity event to raise funds?" Brianna gazed at Dirk with anticipation on her lovely face. Leopold had no doubt Dirk would accommodate the future pride queen.

Leopold observed his mate in silence as Dirk contemplated her request. Brianna fidgeted in her chair, seemingly worried about his cousin's response. She didn't need to be, Dirk wouldn't let his alpha down.

Dirk's lips curved into a sly smile. "I don't know why I hadn't thought of this before. Let's do it up right. A black-tie event, like the Met Gala. An exclusive yearly event, with a different guest list each time. Actors, directors, producers, and musicians who can also perform."

"I love that idea. Thank you." Brianna's smile was a mile wide.

"I think it'll be an amazing event. We'll do a red carpet, get the press there. We could have it here. The first Thursday in September. The weather will still be nice." Dirk suggested.

Leopold loved the idea, and the visibility the event and their cause would garner. He'd happily donate the event space at the hotel. Why was Brianna frowning?

"So many of our current donors are individuals with smaller donations. I'd love for them to participate in some way. Their donations matter too." She pursed her lips while contemplating the dilemma. "What if we held a drawing of the current donors and selected five. They could bring a plus one if they wanted."

It spoke volumes about her character that his mate had such a giving spirit. A sense of fairness and inclusion. She'd make the perfect mate for him. His cock twitched in his pants anticipating what was in store for the future.

Over dessert they ironed out the details of their upcoming charity gala. He and Dirk would cover the winner's first-class air fare and accommodations at LVH Luxe. Their prize included two tickets to the gala on Thursday, a private tour of the New York sanctuary on Friday, and a night on the town at The Lion's Den Manhattan on Saturday before they returned home on Sunday. Things were looking up for this club and sanctuary expansion project. If he could persuade his mate to give him a chance, he'd be a happy lion.

Several hours later Leopold found himself at home on the couch, with his cuddly black kitten on his lap purring her heart out. He hoped one day soon he helped Brianna get over her fear of cats to meet Prissy. She was a good little girl, and he was certain she'd win over his mate if given the chance. He pet her soft, vibrating body and smiled down at his little girl.

"So, you're sure your father and I will get an invitation to the gala?" He'd called his mother and conferenced in Chloe to whine about his lack of romantic progress with Brianna. They seemed to only care about the gala guest list.

"And me too?" Chloe chimed in.

He sighed and leaned back in frustration. "Yes, of course. You'll be invited every year if the first gala goes well. Brianna suggested alternating our other high profile family members to be fair." They had family and pride members who held various state and federal government office and executive corporate positions, which would bring much needed attention and donations to the cause.

"We'll need to shop for dresses, Chloe," his mother said, ignoring him.

"Heck yes, we do. Let's invite Brianna to join us," his sister suggested.

"Great idea, honey."

Damn it. He needed to steer the conversation back to him and not party plans. "Ladies. The charity gala isn't the reason I called you. What am I supposed to do about my mate? I thought introducing her to Dirk would have swayed her a little in my direction. But she seemed more inclined to keep me at arm's length than she did before."

"Son, these grand gestures won't help. Take it from me. Humans don't understand the mating pull. I was so confused at first. You need a more subtle approach. Don't forget she just went through a horrible divorce."

"Mom's right. Grayson's still bothering her. I can hear her at home, telling him to leave her alone when he calls her. He's such a jerk."

Leopold growled. He should take care of Grayson once and for all. What was wrong with him? He'd lost, game over. Brianna was and would always belong to *him*.

"Show her from your *heart*, not over-the-top gestures, what a wonderful man you are. Make it personal. I assure you; she *will* come around. The mating bond won't fail you, in plenty of time to meet the elders' deadline."

He couldn't care less about the elders or their bullshit deadline, but Leopold hoped his mother was right.

Chapter Five

Taking his mother's advice to heart, literally, Leopold checked the fifteen-pound turkey baking in his oven. It wouldn't be much longer before it'd be ready. The cheesy au gratin potatoes and lemon, garlic, and olive oil green beans were just about done. Nothing too fancy, but hearty and what he knew would be delicious. His mother's homemade strawberry shortcake was in the refrigerator for dessert.

His parents had just arrived. Brianna, Chloe and her friend and current boy-toy Mason Walker were due any minute. He'd tucked Prissy safely in the sunroom with plenty of fresh water and food. He wouldn't take any chances by scaring Brianna on her first visit.

A visit which Brianna had initially declined as seeming too much like an intimate date, until Chloe had assured her it was a casual *family* dinner, not dinner alone with Leopold. He owed his sister big time.

When the doorbell rang, his stomach flipped. He sensed and scented his mate at the front door. At her future home. *Their* future home. His lion paced, anxious to see her.

His mother had already let his mate in and was shaking her hand, and both of them were smiling warmly, by the time he reached the front door. *Off to a good start.* Dressed simply in black slacks and a lavender silk blouse, Brianna was enticing nonetheless, and his pulse hitched. She held what appeared to be a burgundy wine carrier bag in one hand. Leopold brushed off a pang of jealousy when his mate allowed his father a friendly kiss on the cheek in the way of a greeting.

Brianna's eyes beamed with happiness when she glanced at him. His spirits soared.

"You look so much like your father. What a resemblance."

Did she consider that a good thing? Stories of his father were legendary. He'd been quite the lady's man before meeting his mother, his fated mate. Dear old Dad hadn't looked at another woman since then, or so Leopold had been told.

She held up her wine bag. "I brought two bottles of Chardonnay. It should pair well with turkey, right?" It was ideal. His mate was perfect.

"Perfect choice, thank you. Let's put it in the refrigerator while we wait on dinner. It shouldn't be much longer."

He led Brianna to the remodeled state-of-the-art kitchen and placed her wine in the refrigerator. Being alone with her made his senses reel, her scent intoxicating. His lion clawed to be set free, but Leopold held back because he had to.

"Let me check on the turkey." A quick inspection revealed it was cooked. He removed it from the oven and set it down to cool.

Brianna's eyes sparkled and a tender smile spread across her face. "It smells wonderful. You really made it yourself?"

His lion nodded in the affirmative. "Oh, ye of little faith. I baked the turkey and made au gratin potatoes and seasoned green beans. Mom brought her homemade strawberry shortcake for dessert. Come, let me show you the house before I carve and we can eat."

"*Meow.*" How had Prissy gotten into the kitchen?

Brianna shrieked and immediately ducked

behind him. He felt her trembling as she clung to him.

"You never said you had a cat. Please. Please get him out of here." She clung tighter and he heard her panting.

"There she is." His mother came into the kitchen apparently looking for Prissy. "Poor thing was locked in the sunroom." She bent down and pet a now purring Prissy who seemed curious about who was hiding behind him.

"*Meow, meow.*"

"Leo, please." Brianna pleaded in a whisper.

"Mom, please bring Prissy back to the sunroom and close the door. Brianna is afraid of cats." Leopold hoped his mother would do as he asked and not make a fuss.

"I'm s-s-sorry, Mariana," Brianna said meekly from behind him.

His mother scooped up his kitten in her arms. "No, I'm the one who's sorry. I didn't know. I'll put her back in the sunroom. Don't worry, dear."

After his mother left the kitchen, Brianna let go of him. Leopold immediately missed her touch. He turned around to find her with her head down, seemingly ashamed and embarrassed.

"Look at me. What happened to make you so afraid? Prissy is a good girl. Gentle, loving and a wonderful cuddler. She'd never hurt you; I assure you." Whatever it was, Leopold would fix it. Brianna was his mate, but Prissy was his little girl. He and the kitten were a package deal.

She nodded sadly and raised her left arm, bending at the elbow. He spotted the faint, healed scars right away. What the hell had happened to his mate?

"I was six, playing with my friends in the alley behind our house in Bay Ridge," Brianna began. "Well, there were a few neighborhood stray cats people used to feed. For the most part they were friendly, but the tabby was kind of mean. We were playing with our dolls and hadn't realized he'd come up behind us. I got startled and accidentally stepped on his tail. He got really upset and ripped up my elbow. My best friend Jilly beat on him with her doll until he ran off. The damage had already been done. I ended up with twenty-five stitches."

He placed a gentle kiss on her elbow. She smiled sadly then lowered her arm and shrugged.

"I'm so sorry, Brianna. You must have been terrified." Thank goodness for her little friend Jilly or her injuries could have been much worse.

"I was. I feel so stupid. It was years ago. I really need to get over it. Hell, I work for The

Lion's Den now. How crazy is that, considering my issues?"

Leopold was grateful when she allowed him to kiss her forehead. Her skin was soft and warm to the touch. "Not stupid at all. Thank you for sharing that with me. You have nothing to fear from little Prissy. I promise. Not that I'm pushing her on you. Just that maybe spending time with her can help you overcome your fears, now as an adult."

His mate nodded, appearing more in control of herself. "Maybe."

"Let me give you a quick tour and then we can eat," he suggested.

A sweet smile graced her lovely face again. "That's a great idea."

His Fifth Avenue home was one of the most notable residences remaining in private hands in the area. It was built by the most sought-after architect in American history, on the finest block of Fifth Avenue; the only block on the Upper East Side where no high-rise apartment would ever be allowed.

The entire block was referred to as the Cook Block, as his home had been originally built for Mr. Henry Cook in 1906. Leopold had the home meticulously restored and completely modern-ized beneath its stately surface which amazingly escaped the ravages of passing tastes and destructive architectural design whims.

It remained an intact masterpiece, irreplaceable, rare, and highly coveted. Just like his mate. He hoped Brianna could envision herself living here. With seven floors and over fifteen thousand square feet, nine bedrooms, and ten full bathrooms, there would be ample room for their future family.

Every modern convenience including an elevator had been added and every system upgraded with an effortless elegance.

The house had a full frontage on Fifth Avenue with glorious views from entertaining rooms with over sixteen-foot ceilings easily topping the trees and wonderful views over Central Park.

There were grand rooms for formal entertaining and cozy rooms for intimate gatherings like their dinner, both with handsome original details, paneling, and lovely park views.

He ended Brianna's tour at the very top of his home, where a marvelous rooftop garden and patio had been built, lifting them high above Central Park with open 180-degree views to the west side skyline and the tippy glass towers of Midtown Manhattan.

Leopold observed her as she admired the

view. "So, what do you think of Mr. Boss Man's big house?"

She turned and faced him, her expression serious. "It's not how big the house is, Leo. It's how happy the home is."

Later, Leopold considered her words as he carved the turkey and spooned the au gratin potatoes and green beans into serving bowls. He'd accomplished much in his nearly forty years, mostly for his family and pride. Some for himself personally. He'd worked incredibly hard to fulfill his obligations, sacrificing his personal life as a result.

Now that he'd met Brianna, his fated mate, he realized how much he'd given up. How much he never knew he'd wanted until now. His woman, a future, a family. The elders' outrageous deadline and threats didn't factor into his desires in the least. Everything was different now.

Seated in the smaller dining room which sat six, he served dinner. He and his mate each sat at the head of the table on either end. His parents flanked Brianna and Chloe and Mason flanked him.

He felt a sense of pride as Brianna seemed to enjoy his cooking.

"You really didn't help Leo with dinner, Mariana?" Brianna asked his mother with amusement in her eyes.

His mother sipped her Chardonnay before she answered. "Absolutely not. My side of the family doesn't come from money."

"I adore the Campbell side of the family, Mom." Leopold assured his mother. They were a loving, hardworking, blue-collar family. Much like Brianna's, from what he'd discerned from her background check.

"Me too," Chloe said.

"Well, my family didn't have help. I wanted Leopold and Chloe to have essential life skills, so I taught them both how to cook, run the vacuum, wash dishes by hand, clean the bathroom and launder their clothes. I wanted to make sure they could take care of themselves and not be a burden on their future mates – spouses. Leopold studied abroad after graduating from Harvard and trained with renowned French chef Pierre Laurent." His mother bragged on him.

Brianna's eyes widened, seemingly impressed. She raised her wine glass and tipped it in his direction. "My compliments to tonight's chef. Everything is delicious."

He'd studied under chef Laurent and could keep his house clean? Brianna assumed Leopold had a household staff considering how busy his work kept him and how large his home was, but knowing he could take care of himself was surprisingly appealing. Grayson had been helpless in the kitchen and at home. He'd expected Brianna to work for him all day *and* keep their five thousand square foot home spotless, too much of a cheapskate to hire someone and give her a break. Brianna had finally had enough, running herself ragged and had hired a cleaning service, which she paid for, the last two years of their marriage.

She shook her head, returning her focus to Leopold's scrumptious meal. The turkey was moist and flavorful. The potatoes and green beans a delicious accompaniment. She glanced around the table and found that other than her and Leopold's mother, their plates were stacked high.

Brianna leaned in toward Mariana. "I've noticed your family has large appetites."

His mother remained silent, and Brianna scolded herself for opening her big mouth. Grayson had told her enough times she needed to keep it shut. She hoped she hadn't insulted the woman's family. Aside from the unfortunate kitten incident earlier, they'd been having such a nice time.

"I know. If I ate like they did, I'd weigh five hundred pounds." She giggled and shook her head. "They've been blessed with fast metabolisms, I suppose."

"I admit, I'm a little jealous," Brianna said before indulging in a hearty bite of cheesy au gratin potatoes. *Well done, Leo.*

Mariana nodded. "Me too, dear. I wanted to thank you for all the wonderful work you've done at The Lion's Den. We have high hopes for the expansion with you leading the charge. And the Fallen Angel drink program for the women? Brilliant idea."

All the men at the table nodded in agreement. Brianna's heart swelled with gratitude for the recognition of her efforts. A far cry from her days at Parlora.

"It's unfortunate that in this day and age a program like the Fallen Angel is needed, but I'm certain the club's female guests are comforted knowing it's available," Leopold's father Willem said. She knew him to be sixty-nine years old, but he could have passed for a man in his mid to late fifties.

"And you're sure we're invited to the charity gala in September? We don't want to interfere with the invitation plan you put together, but we're thrilled." Mariana's bright blue eyes sparkled with excitement.

Brianna really liked Leopold's mother. She saw a lot of Mariana in her son. Leopold's family were worth nearly two hundred billion dollars, his personal net worth at twelve billion, but he also had blue collar roots, just as *she* did.

"Of course you are. You're his parents." Brianna glanced at Chloe who appeared to be listening with great interest. "And sister. If our first gala goes well, we'll alternate the other prominent members of the family every year, adding to the event's exclusivity and create the buzz and visibility we need to increase donations."

In addition to international superstar Dirk Van Curen, Leopold's family included state and federal congress and senate politicians, corporate leaders, high ranking military including Leopold's Uncle Hendrick, a four-star army general, and supermodel Mariska Baeten, their family's driver's youngest sibling, to name a few. Prominent members of the Van Housen and their related families abounded, to say the least.

Mariana squealed in delight. Leopold nodded in acknowledgement, a slow smile lifting his kissable lips, causing the pit of Brianna's stomach to tingle.

"I'm so glad. Chloe and I wondered if you'd like to join us and go gown shopping? The gala will be here before you know it. And it leaves us plenty of time for alterations."

Brianna didn't stand a chance against the hopeful expressions on Mariana's and Chloe's faces. With all the work she'd been doing with Dirk and Leopold organizing the event, press releases, licensing for the small donor drawing, and the other countless planning activities, she hadn't given much thought to what she'd wear.

"Your dress, shoes, and all the accessories you need should go on your corporate credit card." Leopold instructed her. She found the authoritative tone of his voice hotter than sin.

"That's not necessary. I can dress myself on my own dime. You should know, you're paying me rather well." Brianna winked at Mariana who nodded back at her.

"True, but it's a corporate event, is it not? Use your corporate credit card."

"Oh! After we get our dresses and we know our colors, we should go to the salon and get our nails and hair done, as a trial run. What do you think?" Chloe was such a sweetheart. Brianna had enjoyed getting to know her over the last few weeks. She couldn't have asked for a better next-door neighbor either.

She glanced across the table at her dinner host, fairly certain how he'd respond. He seemed so regal, now wearing a suit jacket like Mason and his father. Brianna never tired of looking at him – the mischievous, sparkling baby blues, thick blond hair she ached to run her fingers through, the aristocratic profile, and his toned musculature. In *her* mind, he was almost beautiful.

He sipped his Chardonnay and then placed the wine glass back down on the table. "Your hair and nails are attending the gala, aren't they? Corporate credit card."

Brianna saluted him to everyone's apparent amusement. "Yes, sir, Mr. Boss Man."

Leopold's father raised his glass. "To our women. They're going to give all the celebrities a run for their money at the gala." Everyone around the table raised their glasses then took a sip of wine. Brianna wasn't technically one of the family's women, but she appreciated the compliment regardless.

Mariana refocused her attention on Brianna. "How are you enjoying being back in New York after so many years in California? Willem and I know of the Reeds from family visits to the west coast. They've done well for themselves with their restaurant chain."

Brianna had been expecting those kinds of questions tonight and had been prepared. Many Van Housen company employees were family or as they referred to them, "allies" of the family. She was an outsider, although they had warmly welcomed her.

"Honestly? I miss my in-laws the most. We were close. Helen helped me renegotiate all the club contracts. She's been wonderful through the ugliness of divorcing her son." Brianna didn't know what she would have done if Grayson's parents had turned on her. He'd made the process unbearable. She was relieved to finally be free.

Mariana's expression turned sympathetic. "Although the circumstances of your return home aren't ideal, perhaps it's a blessing in disguise. Opportunities you hadn't anticipated might present themselves."

Brianna immediately thought of Leopold. She hadn't anticipated him. Was he the opportunity Mariana was hinting at? She wasn't convinced it was one she should take but couldn't help wondering "what if" anyway.

"What about your family? They must be thrilled you're back," Mariana said.

That was an understatement. They'd warned her early on about Grayson, but she'd been stubborn and hadn't listened, insisting she knew best. She'd paid the price in so many ways and was working hard to put the ugly experience behind her.

"They are. My mother passed away from lung cancer when I was ten." Mariana reached over and squeezed Brianna's hand gently. A sweet motherly gesture she welcomed. Chloe held a hand to her heart, having already heard Brianna's life story highlight reel.

"I have three older brothers, two are married with children. One of them married my best friend Jilly, they have a six-month-old son. My oldest brother Vito lives with my father and has space in the finished attic. He runs his plumbing business from there. In fact, we have Sunday family dinners twice a month, now that grandchildren have joined the family. I'll visit with them next Sunday."

"I'd enjoy meeting them if they wouldn't mind me inviting myself." Leopold eyed her expectantly, while his family remained silent.

Her ex had considered the Palermos low class, not good enough for the likes of him. He'd never wanted to visit New York or invite them to visit them in California. Although Leopold may have blue collar roots, it wasn't how he'd been raised, and far from how he'd lived his entire life. He'd lived a life of wealth and privilege. If she indulged him and brought him to her father's place, he might finally let go of the idea they should be together. The thought made her heart hurt, even though she believed it was for the best.

"Sure. Why not?" She could manage a few hours with him and her family. She hoped.

Brianna washed and dried her hands in the powder room after devouring Mariana's homemade strawberry shortcake. Leopold had prepared perfect cappuccinos for everyone. He'd been a considerate and attentive host. The complete opposite of Grayson, who had felt entitled and expected everyone to wait on him hand and foot. She vowed not to compare the two men again. Grayson was the past and needed to stay there. If only he'd leave her the hell alone.

She turned toward the closed door when she heard what sounded like scratching. What the heck? Was Leopold scratching at the door?

Brianna slowly opened the door. Leopold wasn't there.

"*Meow.*" Prissy stood there, looking up at her with her intense blue eyes, holding up one of her paws as if she was waving at her. Brianna trembled in fear, but still found the kitten adorable.

She slowly lifted her hand and waved back. "Hi, Prissy. Leo?" Did he know Prissy wasn't in the sunroom? She remained still, hoping Leopold would come to the rescue soon before Prissy possibly hurt her.

"There you both are," Leopold said and scooped up the kitten in his arms.

"*Meeeoww.*" Prissy rubbed her head against Leopold's neck. Brianna found it sweet yet terrifying, although he seemed perfectly calm.

"She's harmless, I promise. Try to pet her, just for a second. Trust me, I won't let anything happen to you."

She did trust him. He wasn't the issue. Years of paralyzing fear was. Brianna stepped forward, hoping to push years of fear away, once and for all. She pet Prissy's head with the tip of her index finger. It was a start. The kitten was soft and warm. She pulled her hand away when she heard and felt the kitten growl at her.

"She's purring, Brianna. She's happy. Content. Pet her a little more. It'll be all right."

Prissy tilted her head to meet Brianna's hand as she stroked the kitten gently. She felt and heard her purrs. Brianna felt tears streaming down her face.

Overwhelmed with emotions, Brianna gently brushed her lips over Leopold's in a tender kiss.

Prissy licked her jaw with her rough kitty tongue. Brianna giggled and ended their much too brief kiss. It was surreal.

Leopold's lips quirked into a grin. "You see? Prissy wanted to get in on the action and give you kisses too. She likes you nearly as much as I do."

Chapter Six

Against her better judgement, Brianna made her way to pick Leopold up for dinner the following Sunday afternoon. *She'd* insisted on driving. *He'd* insisted she take her company car. Knowing her father, he'd encourage Leopold to sample his homemade wine, which was incredibly strong and grappa, a pomace type brandy, distilled from the winemaking leftovers, which was even stronger. She never drank either.

She'd second guessed herself all week about this family dinner at her father's place. Would her family assume she and Leopold were dating? The few intense kisses they'd shared hadn't really meant anything, had they?

Brianna speculated that after he'd spent time with her average, working-class family today, he'd lose interest in pursuing her. The thought made her sad and she chastised herself for being so indecisive about him. What was it about him that intrigued her so? Aside from his obvious good looks. It was more than that, she just couldn't put her finger on it. She couldn't deny she was drawn to him.

As she approached Cook Block, she contemplated what it would hurt if she and Leopold had an affair. Had a little fun. They were both consenting adults and were clearly attracted to each other. What was the real harm in it? She'd earned herself a little fun after what she'd gone through with Grayson in California. It was *her* time now. Brianna's employment contract was ironclad, ensuring her job wouldn't be in jeopardy either way.

Brianna pulled up to Leopold's house on Fifth Avenue. She'd decided not to straighten her hair like she normally did, enjoying her natural curls for a change. It was another thing Grayson had no say over any longer. And she'd chosen a pair of jeans that made her ass look good, though it shouldn't have mattered. The car smelled sweet with her homemade cannoli bars in the backseat for dessert. Would anyone notice if she had one before she got to her father's place?

She chuckled to herself, finding Leopold

outside holding Prissy, with two cases of Peroni beer on the ground beside him. A gift her father and brothers would surely appreciate. He was just as gorgeous in khakis and a light blue dress shirt as he was when he wore a designer suit. Damn him.

She exited her car, and cautiously approached the man and his kitten. Leopold's eyes smoldered as he slowly raked his eyes over her body. Heat whispered through her veins. He was potent without even saying a word.

"*Meeoow.*"

"I agree, Prissy. Brianna looks beautiful with her hair curly instead of straightened." Heat flared in Leopold's eyes as he gave her another slow once over.

Before Brianna spontaneously combusted on Fifth Avenue in front of his neighbors, she summoned her courage and pet his sweet little black kitten, recognizing the sound and feel of her purrs. She was incredibly proud of herself for slowly getting over her fear of cats. One day soon, she'd ask to hold Prissy.

His lips curved with a proud smile. "Well done. Let me get her inside and we can go."

When Brianna made to grab the cases of Peroni, Leopold slid her a warning glance. "I'll put them in the car."

Brianna blew out a breath and rolled her eyes. She waved at Prissy before getting back in her car. Within a minute Leopold had loaded the beer in her backseat, buckled himself into the passenger seat, and they were on their way to her father's house. She prayed their visit wouldn't be a mistake.

Her telephone chimed with a text message when they had about ten minutes left to their commute. Brianna hoped it wasn't Grayson. She'd grown weary of his frequent and pointless contact. She'd placed her phone in one of the front seat cup holders.

"Would you mind checking the text for me, Leo? It could be my father. They might need something for dinner, and we can pick it up on our way."

He grabbed her phone and checked the display. "It's Leopold."

"Right." He was such fun to tease.

He grunted and her stomach knotted. Was there a problem?

"It's from Vito and just says College Fuck."

Brianna knew from reviewing the naughty drink recipes with the Manhattan club mixologist that a College Fuck was made with vodka, kiwi strawberry Snapple, orange juice, and ice. "Ever since I started managing Parlora, my brother Vito became even more of a smart ass and at Sunday dinners, he makes a different naughty drink for everyone. Looks like College Fucks are on the menu today."

Leopold nodded, seemingly lost in thought for a moment. "There's nothing like a shot of Cunnilingus to brighten up a person's day, I always say."

Heat crept up Brianna's neck and ears, and her core dampened. Based on his kisses, she speculated Leopold might be skilled in that area. She couldn't recall the ingredients of that particular drink though.

"What is it?" she asked.

He raised a brow and a wicked smile claimed his lips. "Sweetheart, I'd be happy to show you exactly what–"

Brianna's cheeks burned hot. "No, Leo. What *ingredients* are in the shot?"

His chuckle made her stomach flip. "It's Leopold. Bailey's Irish Cream, Peach Schnapps, pineapple juice and whipped cream."

It sounded delicious. Not nearly as good as Leopold going down on her, but that wasn't an option at the moment. They arrived at her father's Colonial in Bay Ridge, Brooklyn before she lost it and jumped him on the side of the road.

She pulled into the shared driveway and turned off the ignition. "You're sure about this? Are you really ready to see how the other half lives?" Brianna offered Leopold one final opportunity to change his mind. It was better than an awkward visit like they'd had to endure with Grayson. She wouldn't put her family through that again. They were good people, deserving of respect and regard.

"What kind of an asshole was that ex-husband of yours? Half of me *is* the other half. I look forward to meeting your family."

Leopold's sincere expression had her wanting to believe him. "You've never actually *lived* that half and you know it."

He nodded, seemingly in agreement. "True. But I'll admit to *you*, I've much preferred the company of the Campbell relatives in New Jersey than the Van Housens in New York. Especially lately."

She wasn't sure what he meant but had no choice but to take his word for it. Her stomach fluttered as they approached her family in the backyard. Vito had his back to them, manning two grills. One with vegetables, the other with what she knew was marinated skirt steaks and boneless chicken thighs. It smelled heavenly, and her stomach growled. She noticed her father in his greenhouse, most likely selecting fresh vegetables for a quick tossed salad.

Brianna didn't have to say much at first. Her brother Dante shook Leopold's hand and happily brought the two cases of beer into the house. Her brother Tommaso (Tommy) greeted them casually as did her sisters-in-law Lara and her best friend Jillian (Jilly). Her ten-year-old nephew Matteo (Matt) was engrossed with a handheld video game and her five-year-old niece Angelica (Angel) was combing her doll's hair as she watched her big brother play his game. A typical Sunday at the Palermos.

When Tommy brought Leopold over to meet Vito, Lara and Jilly flanked her as she'd expected.

"Holy shit," Jilly whispered.

"Damn, isn't *he* a tall, cool glass of Rosé or what?" Lara discreetly fanned herself, driving the point home.

While Brianna agreed Leopold was, it didn't sit well that her sisters-in-law thought so, even if they were married to her brothers. The unexpected twinge of jealousy didn't sit well.

"He sure puts Grayson to shame. He looks like a Viking or something. I bet he looks hot in a kilt." Jilly's comment made *Brianna* hot just thinking about it. Of course, he'd look hot in a damn kilt. He *always* looked hot.

"Vikings didn't wear kilts." Brianna stated. "They most likely wore linen or wool tunics and trousers."

Lara and Jilly looked at each other and laughed. Brianna's face heated.

"They say *real* men don't wear anything under their kilts," Lara teased.

"Leopold strikes me as a *real* man. Wouldn't you say Bree?" Jilly winked at her and giggled.

Brianna excused herself from her cackling sisters-in-law when her father exited his greenhouse with salad fixings in a linen bag. She gently took Leopold by the arm and led him to her dad.

"Dad, this is Leopold Van Housen. He's my new boss."

Her father, now seventy, white haired, was still in good health and mentally sharp. He beamed up at them and extended his hand.

"Good to meet you, Leepold. Welcome to my home."

Leopold's friendly smile warmed Brianna's heart. It would be all right. She'd been nervous for no reason.

"It's Leopold, Dad," Brianna corrected him.

"I said Leepold, Brianna."

"Dad. Leo. Pold."

"*Si*. Leepold. I said that."

"No, Dad. Listen. It's—"

Leopold squeezed her hand. Her subtle cue to shut the hell up she assumed. It wasn't as if *she'd* ever called him Leopold herself.

"You like some fresh vegetables to take home?" His Italian accent was heavy and charming, but easy to understand. Brianna's father gestured to his greenhouse.

Leopold nodded eagerly. "Yes. Thank you, sir."

"Eh, call me Aldo." He handed his vegetable bag to Brianna. *"Puoi preparare l'insalata per tutti noi?"*

She stole a quick glance in Leopold's direction and her lips curved into an easy smile.

God, she's beautiful.

"Sure, Dad. Salad coming up."

Aldo led Leopold into the warm greenhouse. The scent of earth and freshly growing food was comforting to him and his lion. His lion enjoyed spending time in nature up at the Claverack estate and splashing in the property's pond. He'd brought Prissy there several times. His lion had taught her how to swim.

"Leepold. Is family name?" Aldo grabbed a large brown paper bag and opened it wide.

"Yes sir, Aldo. It's my great grandfather's name. From the Netherlands."

"*Buono, buono.* So, what you like?" Aldo gestured around the greenhouse's bounty.

"*Se ti senti più a tuo agio a parlare in Italiano.*" Leopold was fluent in several languages, including Italian. There was no reason for Aldo to struggle with English in order to communicate with him.

Aldo raised his brows and chuckled. "Is fine. I like to practice my English. My boys, they make this for me ten years ago. So, we have fresh vegetables all year."

"I think it's wonderful. Fresh is always better than store bought. Can I have some plum tomatoes, zucchini, eggplant, and green peppers?" He thought of inviting Brianna over, *alone*, for a delicious stir fry dinner.

"*Si.* I love to garden. Sometimes a man need time alone. To think. So much noise in the world, you know?" Aldo filled the bag with Leopold's vegetables, appearing to select what he considered the best his garden had to offer.

So much noise, especially now. Leopold understood completely. He spent time alone when he could, on his rooftop patio for that very reason. To get away from all the noise.

"I do. If I had the time, I'd love my own garden."

Aldo handed Leopold his filled bag. He looked forward to inviting Brianna over for dinner again.

"Ah, but too many responsibilities. I know about that too." Aldo's expression turned serious.

Brianna's father knew all too well. His beloved wife Rosa Santoro had been snatched away from him much too soon, leaving him to raise four children on his own. From what Leopold could tell, he and he assumed with help from both the Palermo and Santoro extended families, did an amazing job.

Leopold boiled with fury and his jaw clenched when his Uncle Hendrick waltzed onto the patio in jeans and an army T-shirt, and a practiced smile on his face. His lion growled, scratching to be set free. What the fuck was *he* doing here? Was he after Brianna? When Vito saw him, his eyes widened and he saluted the general in perfect form.

Aldo nudged his shoulder. "*Chi è questo?*"

Leopold shot Hendrick a venomous look. "*Mio zio.*"

"At ease, Vito. It's a family cookout." Hendrick dropped his salute and shook Vito's hand reminding him of a politician. In some respects, he suspected his uncle was, at his rank in the military.

Hendrick and Aldo shook hands. "It's a pleasure to meet you, Mr. Palermo. I'm General Hendrick Van Housen, Leopold's uncle. I hope I'm not intruding. I was in the area."

"Welcome to my home. We have plenty. You stay for dinner, *si*?"

"I'd love to, thank you. What's in the bag, nephew?" Hendrick wasn't getting his hands on his fresh vegetables. No way, no how. They were hand-picked especially for *him* by his future father-in-law. He clutched the bag against his hip and glared at his uncle.

Aldo's face lit up. "You like some fresh vegetables from my greenhouse? I get you some. No worry." Aldo dashed back inside the greenhouse.

Vito glanced between him and his uncle, seemingly confused. "General, you're Leopold's uncle? How can that be?"

Hendrick shrugged. "I was a later in life child for Leopold's grandparents. There are fewer years between him and I than there are between me and his father, my older brother."

Aldo returned, all smiles with a bag for Hendrick. One not quite as full as his own. Juvenile as it seemed, that pleased him and his lion very much.

"Everything's ready, so your timing is perfect, general." Vito turned to the grills and grabbed a set of silver tongs.

Hendrick shoved his bag at Leopold and went to help. "We leave them, Leepold. I think Vito excited to meet him. We go inside and get the table ready."

Leopold sighed, knowing Aldo was probably right. Perhaps his uncle had stopped by to help him score points with his mate's family. It wasn't necessary. He was perfectly charming and likeable without Hendrick's help.

He followed Aldo inside to the dining room. Leopold's mouth watered inhaling the delicious aroma of what he believed was some sort of baked pasta dish. His lion licked his chops wanting in on the action. *Another time, buddy.*

Brianna, Lara, and Jilly had the table set, salad and crusty bread in the center. He placed the vegetable bags on the floor in the corner. Brianna's brother Dante was cooing over his and Jilly's six-month-old son DJ in between pulls of the Peroni Leopold had brought. Her brother Tommy was settling Angel and Matt down in between pulls of his. He couldn't help but smile. One day his and Brianna's children would sit at this table.

Over a delicious meal beginning with Brianna's recipe for Italian sausage filled lasagna pockets, perfectly cooked skirt steak, chicken thighs and grilled vegetables, Leopold learned about his future in-laws in ways his mate's background check couldn't detail.

Aldo's homemade red wine and peach grappa were quite tasty and were considered very strong for a human. No match for a shifter's metabolism though. Leopold, and he assumed his uncle felt welcomed. The Palermos were kind and gracious and he couldn't fault Vito for being a fanboy toward Hendrick. Leopold's own personal feelings aside, his uncle was a patriot and had served the country honorably.

Lara and her friends were skilled hair stylists and were saving to open their own salon in a neighborhood where their husband's felt it was safe enough for their wives to close up alone at night. If he could only get Brianna to consent to their mating, Leopold would happily solve that problem for them.

Vito had retired from the marines after over twenty years of honorable service and started All American Vets HVAC, HVAC installation, maintenance, and plumbing. Aldo, a union plumber had helped his oldest son get started. They employed veterans, did quality work at fair prices, and offered military families and veterans discounts.

Aldo and his close friends and brothers were all skilled and union tradesmen from plumbing to masonry, carpentry, and flooring. They'd renovated and updated their kid's homes in the neighborhood at cost, including Tommy's and Dante's. They were a hardworking, close-knit group and Leopold was proud to one day join their family.

Hendrick had been pleasant enough, but Leopold couldn't help but wonder why he was underfoot all of the sudden. "Out of curiosity uncle, shouldn't you be in Syria, Libya or some other place that needs your expert command?"

Vito frowned at him, but Leopold couldn't worry about that. Something was going on and as alpha, he needed to know.

Hendrick shrugged. "I'm trying to use up quite a bit of accrued leave."

"Since when do you care about using leave?" Not that Leopold kept tabs on Hendrick, but he'd spent much of his career in the field, engaged.

"Leo." Brianna glared at him without blinking. Shit, he'd upset his mate in front of her family. Damn it.

"Is Leepold," Aldo corrected.

Vito answered before Hendrick could. "Since he's planning to retire, isn't that right, general?"

Retire? Hendrick was only fifty-three. No, that couldn't be right. Uncle Dearest was up to something. Leopold was almost certain of it.

Hendrick shrugged and sipped his peach grappa. "Vito's right. There is a shelf life for generals I'm afraid. I've reached it."

"What does a retired general do next?" Lara asked as she wiped Angel's mouth with a napkin.

"He could become Defense Secretary." Vito explained.

"But he has to be a civilian for at least seven years." Leopold wasn't completely ignorant of the process.

Brianna's eyes darkened and she kicked him under the table. Fuck. "Really?"

Hendrick chuckled. "It's true, don't be upset with Leopold."

"Unless Congress approves a waiver before then. I believe they would," Vito clarified.

Hendrick nodded. "Also true. I have options. Between us, I've been offered a seven-figure advance to write my memoirs. I can consult and the speaking and lecture circuits are quite lucrative for someone at my level. I can always ask my dear nephew for a job. I believe I've proven myself to be an effective leader."

Everyone around the table chuckled. Hendrick's friendly smile implied he didn't mean any harm by his last comment. But Leopold felt for the man, despite his personal feelings about him. His uncle didn't need the money, but it wasn't always about the money. It was about contributing, about feeling useful, needed, and valued.

Conversation flowed freely after Hendrick's career confession. They'd enjoyed Brianna's sweet cannoli bars and espresso.

The kids had excused themselves from the table and ran in and out of the room as children that age tended to do. Angel ran back in, holding chewing gum in her hand and Leopold watched, as if in slow motion, her trip near his chair. He caught her before she fell, but she grabbed onto his hair in a panic, to brace herself.

"Uh oh," the little girl whispered and stared at his head.

Heat burned his cheeks and his stomach fluttered as he touched his hair where Angel stared. He tugged at the gooey gum stuck in his thick locks.

"My mane! How could you be so careless?" Leopold hollered. His lion roared.

The little girl's eyes filled with tears, making

him feel like an ass. "I'm so...sorry. I didn't mean to."

"Stop pulling at it, Leo. You'll make it worse," Brianna said standing up looking down at the damage.

Angel ran out of the room in hysterics, her big brother following close behind. They'd had such a lovely afternoon until *this*.

"Come on, nephew. It's only hair." Hendrick sounded calm, but his brows were furrowed and he was biting his lip. He ran his fingers through his own perfect hair. He knew for a fact his uncle wouldn't want gum stuck in *his* hair either.

Lara joined Brianna to examine the mess. "It's fine. I can cut the gum out and blend the hair around it."

Was she insane? Cut his hair? His precious mane? "Absolutely not. It's just candy, surely you can pick it out."

Vito brought over a jar of peanut butter. Leopold had changed his mind about the Palermos. They were all insane. Now was not the time for a fucking snack.

"Picking at it will make it worse. Peanut butter will dissolve the gum." Vito informed everyone.

"How you know this?" Aldo's tone was clipped. Leopold needed to diffuse the situation as quickly as he could. Get this visit back on pleasant footing. He heard Angel crying in the next room. *Damn it.*

Brianna scooped out some peanut butter with her fingers and began working it into the stuck gum. Lara followed suit. "Because when I was five Vito stuck gum in my hair and peanut butter is how he got it out."

Leopold remained silent. Brianna and Lara worked on his hair while Aldo scolded his eldest son for being so mean to his younger sister when he should have known better at fifteen years of age. What a shitshow.

"You have the most soft, thick hair. What hair-care products do you use," Lara asked as she wiped her hands with a dishtowel.

He had an amazing mane – head of hair. He already knew that. Were they finished? Was the gum dissolved?

He clamped down on his anger. She and Brianna were doing their best to help him. "Thank you. I've been using Oribe since 2009."

"I've never heard of them," Brianna said as she wiped her own hands.

"That's because you can't afford them. We don't even carry them at the salon I work at. I'd love to carry the line someday when we open our own shop though. Come with me so I can wash the residue out. I'm sorry but you'll have to settle for grocery store brand."

He sighed in relief. No harm done. Leopold followed Lara to the bathroom and allowed her to wash the side of his head the gum had been stuck on. She had a gentle touch and was thorough. After a quick blow dry of the wet area, Leopold ran his hand through his thick, undamaged hair, and then kissed Lara on the cheek.

"Thank you for your help. Now, there's a little girl I need to speak with right away." It was time to make things right and salvage his visit.

He found Angel on the plastic covered couch in the living room wiping her damp eyes. Matt had his arm around her shoulder trying to comfort her. He shot Leopold a furious glance when he noticed him come into the room. *I deserve it.*

When Leopold knelt in front of her, she squeezed her eyes shut. Poor thing. His heart ached for the pain he'd caused her. His lion whined in agony.

"Look at me Angel," Leopold whispered.

"Only friends and family can call her that," Matt spat out.

He couldn't fault the boy for defending his little sister. Leopold had his own to protect.

"Angelica, I want you to know that I'm not angry with you for what happened," he began.

She opened her eyes, her sadness evident. "Because Mommy and *Zia* Brianna got the gum out with the peanut butter?"

"No, sweetie. Even if your mommy had to cut my hair, it would have been all right because I know it was an accident. I was so wrong to act the way I did." Leopold swallowed hard. "I'm a little bit of a baby about my hair. You understand, don't you? You have such beautiful hair yourself. Please accept my apology for losing my temper?"

He sensed the rest of the family in the room behind him. Everyone remained silent as they awaited Angel's reply.

She scooted off the couch, and to his surprise, hugged him tight. She smelled sweet, like powder and baby shampoo. Leopold hoped he and Brianna would have little girls one day.

"I do. And you can call me Angel." Thank God. The rest of Brianna's family cheered and applauded.

"I wish I could make it up to you, but I'm not sure how." What would impress a five-year old girl?

"I think I have an idea, if you want to hear it," his Uncle Hendrick said.

Chapter Seven

Leopold felt victorious as Brianna guided her car out of her father's driveway. He'd taken Hendrick's idea of inviting Brianna's family to The Lion's Den to meet the animals and made it several times better. He'd suggested Angel and Matt invite three of their closest friends and their parents for a fun and educational afternoon the following Saturday. They'd meet the "trained, wild animals" who were actually his pride members, and enjoy a buffet lunch afterwards before the club opened for adult patrons. Matt in particular had been overjoyed by the idea. Leopold seemed to have won him over.

With a sly smile on his face, he used his cell phone to place some important orders he knew the Palermo women would love. Including little Miss Angel. In his opinion, things were looking up and he couldn't have been more pleased. He'd successfully smoothed things over with Angel and left Aldo's home with his bag of fresh vegetables and bottles of homemade red wine and peach grappa.

Brianna craned her neck, trying to sneak a peek at what he was doing as she led them through Bay Ridge and back to Manhattan. "What are you doing over there, all full of yourself, Leo?"

He moved his phone away from prying eyes. He was just about finished ordering. "It's Leopold. And you'll find out soon enough."

"Right. I can't believe you could tell Jilly was expecting again. I hate having to sit on the news for four more weeks until she reaches her third trimester," Brianna said, smiling brightly.

He'd scented the new mother was expecting upon meeting her. And although he'd learned she'd miscarried twice before carrying baby DJ to term, the two-month-old girl she was carrying was strong. He was optimistic Jilly wouldn't miscarry again.

"She had that pregnancy glow. I'm surprised no one else picked up on it. It seemed obvious to me." He wasn't able to admit how he'd actually known. Not yet. Jilly and Brianna had exchanged a look he hadn't been able to decipher when she'd mentioned her previous miscarriages and he hadn't wanted to pry about something so personal and traumatic.

They drove in companiable silence, enjoying the early evening warm weather.

"Thank you for indulging the kids, my family, and their friends next Saturday. Angel was fine with only your apology. She's a good girl. I know things got tense for a little while there." Brianna's expression grew serious as she drove into Manhattan.

"It's fine, really. I'm happy to do it. You know what they say, it's not a party until someone gets gum stuck in their hair and a little girl cries." He was grateful they'd been able to move past the unfortunate gum incident quickly and to everyone's satisfaction. Hendrick's unexpected visit had turned out to be helpful after all.

Brianna snorted and shook her head. He grew melancholy as she turned onto Cook Block and closer to his house. He didn't want the day to end.

She turned off the ignition when they reached his place. "Need some help bringing everything in?" Brianna's cheeks flushed a warm pink, and her penetrating gaze searched his face.

He'd easily manage without her help, though he suspected that wasn't why she'd asked. The scent of her desire filled his nostrils and anticipation pulsed through him.

Brianna followed him inside the house and into the kitchen, remaining quiet. A low and pleasant hum warmed his body. After they'd placed the vegetable bag and alcohol bottles on the kitchen counter, she stood back, leaning against it, faced him and sighed. Her eyes caressed him, and the pulse on her neck fluttered. She looked up at him with a quizzical expression.

Aching to touch her, Leopold brushed a soft, wavy lock of her hair behind her ear.

"This is such a bad idea, Leo."

He smiled down at her. She was wrong, of course. "It's Leopold, and I disagree. I think it's an extraordinary idea."

His finger traced the delicate softness of her plump lower lip and then he lifted her up onto the counter. Her sexy giggle made his cock throb. His lion moaned to be set free and claim his mate, not understanding the need for restraint and consent. *Not yet. Soon.* He hoped.

Leopold nibbled on the pulsing hollow at the base of Brianna's throat where he'd eventually mark and claim her, hoping to temporarily appease his animal. Her shutter drove him insane with need.

"I know we're just having some fun, but I don't want to create any problems or drama between you and Kaylee."

He didn't want to discuss Kaylee, especially now, and especially since there was nothing to discuss. He and Kaylee were a non-issue. He should have fired her and sent her back to her parents when he'd had the chance considering how badly she'd been treating his mate. He'd hadn't done it in front of Brianna's subordinates as to not undermine her.

Leopold's lips pressed against hers, then gently covered her mouth. Their sweet kiss sang through his veins. "No drama or problems. I assure you. You're so much more than fun to me. I already told you I've been yours since the moment we met."

"You can't say things like that to me. I can't give you what you want." She made to hop off the counter, but Leopold stopped her.

"You've already given me everything." His demanding lips met hers in a toe-curling kiss that left him breathless. Brianna pulled him closer, her lips soft and searching. She tugged on his shirt. He obliged by removing it and tossing it aside.

Her fingertips seared his skin when she explored his chest and abdomen.

He unzipped her form-fitting jeans and wrangled them off, along with her purple lace panties. The smell of Brianna's arousal tickled his nose. He spread her legs and ran a finger along her wet slit until he reached her swollen clit and she trembled.

Leopold kissed Brianna with a hunger he'd never experienced before and worked her sensitive nub until she clutched at his hair and came apart in his arms, gasping for breath. His lion roared in victory for pleasing their mate.

He quickly unbuckled his belt and unzipped his pants, unable to wait another minute to fuck his one and only. He scooted her to the edge of the counter, and she wrapped her legs around his hips.

Leopold teased her entrance and felt her pussy wet and ready for him. Brianna spread her legs wider, eager for him. Her silky heat captured his cock as he thrust inside her. She was absolute perfection, snug and slick. Made for him.

Her pussy wrapped around him like a warm blanket as he fucked her hard and deep. This was where he belonged. With her, in her, surrounded by her. Always.

Brianna shuddered and shook as he took what

belonged to him, heat jolting through him. He pistoned in and out of her, her moans of delight encouraging him. He continued fucking her with long, strong thrusts, pulling out and then driving back into her tight heat. Leopold tried to steady his racing heart with a few deep breaths, but it was no use. He happily surrendered to the power of his mate.

His spine tingled when her pussy walls clamped down around his thick shaft. He slipped his hand between their joined bodies and rubbed her clit until they both climaxed together, Leopold coming in pulses and spirts deep inside her. *Mate. Cubs.* His lion was overjoyed at the prospect of procreating. *Shit.* He should have taken Brianna to his bedroom where the condoms were.

He kissed her warm, sweat dampened forehead. "I'm sorry. I was impatient to have you. The condoms are in my bedroom."

She looked at him with pleasure-glazed eyes, not seeming upset. "It's fine. I'm on the pill, and I've been tested."

Leopold should have been relieved but instead found himself disappointed. "I've been tested too. I'd never hurt you. I hope you know that." Shifters couldn't get sick or catch STD's, but he couldn't tell Brianna that yet.

Her angelic smile made his heart swell. He picked her up off the counter and brought her up to his bedroom and gently placed her on his bed like the treasure she was. He'd fucked her again twice before they fell asleep entangled in each other's arms.

He awoke several hours later, still holding his mate when he felt Prissy purring at the foot of the bed. He'd never slept better or felt more at peace in his life. This was what being mated meant. He wished he'd met Brianna sooner and not because of the elders' threats and deadline.

He glanced at the nightstand clock when Brianna stirred. It was just after seven Monday morning. Leopold supposed they should get up. He'd make them breakfast. Mates did that for each other, didn't they?

Leopold had come to terms with the revelation that Brianna was on birth control. He'd concluded that getting her pregnant now, without her full knowledge of who he was and what they were to each other, would have caused more problems than solved them. Last night had been an important first step toward receiving her consent to their mating.

He realized she was awake when she stiffened in his arms. He sensed her panic, her doubts. He wondered if she could sense his ease and joy.

Reluctantly, he let her go and she sat up on the bed, holding the sheet against her luscious tits.

She seemed surprised, but not afraid when she noticed Prissy at the end of the bed. "Oh. Good morning little girl." Prissy approached Brianna purring loudly and laid down across her lap, eager for affection.

Brianna's smile lit up the room. She carefully, but confidently pet his kitten while she purred to her heart's content and stretched across his mate's lap. He was proud Brianna seemed to be getting over her fear of cats.

I'll go start breakfast for us. Come down when you're ready." He slipped out of bed and into a pair of black silk lounge pants.

"Leo."

"It's Leopold." He adored her sass and independence. Hell, he adored everything about her.

"Right. Look, about last night. We were just having some fun. And as much as I enjoyed it, it's not going to lead anywhere. I'm not looking for anything serious." Her slight frown implied she may not have truly believed what she claimed. He knew their bond would eventually win out, regardless of her current proclamation.

He gave Brianna a quick peck on the cheek and Prissy a little rub under her chin, the kitten eating up all the early morning attention.

"You don't have to be so definitive about it. You never know what might happen."

Late Tuesday afternoon Brianna rolled her carryon bag into the Presidential suite on the thirtieth floor of the LVH Luxe Hotel Chicago O'Hare. She'd been greeted by attentive staff with warm, welcoming smiles. Considering her flight had been upgraded to a first-class seat unbeknownst to her, the room upgrade hadn't been much of a surprise. Mr. Boss Man had obviously been busy behind the scenes for her first club-related business trip.

She hadn't been sure of what to expect from Leopold's luxury boutique hotel chain. The stylish property was a contemporary interpretation of his family's northwestern European heritage, and the chic lobby-level lounge had a sultry atmosphere.

As described to her at check-in, her suite was nearly thirteen hundred square feet with a greenhouse design that provided an abundance of natural light. The king size feather bed was buried under multiple layers of crisp, well-appointed Frette linens. Tucked away in the marble bathroom was a glass shower and separate jetted tub. A little time in the tub sounded heavenly before bed.

Awaiting her on the living room table was a fresh bouquet of light peach-colored Zelmira lilies. She eagerly plucked the card out of the plastic holder placed in the center of the sweet-smelling blooms. There was also a gift basket of some sort on the white leather couch.

A real king knows how to take care of his queen. Tears welled up in her eyes and she placed the card back in its holder. She kept reminding herself that Grayson had been attentive and sweet at first too. Brianna believed Leopold wasn't anything like her jerk of an ex-husband but was too afraid to take any chances. She needed to stay strong. Protect her heart. A casual fling was one thing. Allowing herself to be vulnerable to the man who was chipping away at the walls around her heart was another.

Her phone rang, startling her from her thoughts about Leopold. It was just as well. Why was Jilly calling her?

"Oh, my God. Did you get a gift basket too?" Jilly gushed when Brianna connected the call.

She approached the gift basket on the white leather couch. What was going on? She put the phone on speaker and peered inside the clear plastic wrapped basket.

"I just got in my room. There's a basket here. Oh. Oribe products?"

"Yep. Lara got a basket too. It's filled with just about everything – hair care, body care and all three fragrances. In full *and* travel sizes. And Bree, he got Angel a basket filled with Hello Bello products. She thinks she's a sophisticated big girl now with her body lotion and lip balm."

Brianna knew from her sisters-in-law Hello Bello was created by married couple and actors Dax Shepard and Kristen Bell. Such generous and thoughtful gifts. A smile tugged at her lips.

"I know the cost of everything is chump change to a man like him, but what a kind gesture, right? Grayson never did anything this nice before. Ever. Even for *you*. Tell me you're getting a little *something*-something from that hunk of a man or I'll jump him myself."

She tilted her head back and bellowed out a hearty laugh. "Watch it or I'll tell Dante you said that. I may or may not have gotten a little *something*-something. A lady never tells," she teased Jilly.

It was Jilly's turn to laugh. They chatted while Brianna changed into leggings and a T-shirt. The family consensus was everyone liked Leopold, billionaire status aside, and they hoped he and Brianna became involved romantically. They believed he was good for her, unlike her ex-husband. Brianna wasn't willing to discuss her misgivings about a possible relationship with Leopold, even with her best friend, but ended her call with Jilly on a friendly note.

Brianna devoured heirloom tomato salad and margherita with prosciutto flatbread in her room for dinner while reviewing the properties she'd visit and evaluate as potential club locations on her laptop. *Well done, Leo. Delicious.*

There were sites to visit the following day in Chicago proper and on Thursday, sites in nearby western suburbs in what was considered the Chicago Metropolitan area or Chicagoland. She made note of each property's advantages and disadvantages in preparation for her viewings with the realtor Leopold had recommended, an ally of the Van Housen family. They had an extensive network of family and allies across the country and the world. And Brianna had thought *her* family was large. It didn't come close to the size of the Van Housen clan.

Brianna shut down her laptop an hour later when she felt confident she was well prepared for the two days ahead. After half listening to several voicemails from Grayson, alternating between begging her to come back to him and being angry she'd left him, she deleted them, the unread texts and blocked all of his numbers on her phone. Finally.

She'd moved on. Had reunited with her family and best friend. Was enjoying the challenges of her new job and felt more like herself than she had in years. She was happily moving forward with her life. If Grayson wanted to remain stuck in the past, that wasn't her problem. He was a grown man and needed to get his shit together. It wasn't her responsibility to do that for him any longer and she was thankful for that.

The knock on the door startled her. Had room service come to pick up her dirty dinner dishes without her having to call? She looked through the peephole and flung the door open.

"Leo?" Brianna bit down a smile and her insides vibrated. She scolded her emotions to calm the hell down.

A wicked smile claimed his lips as he stood in the hallway, impeccable as he always was in a designer suit. Damn, but she was thrilled to see him.

"It's Leopold."

"Right. Are you here to check up on me?" If he was uncertain about her abilities during this trip, it would crush her. She'd been second guessed her entire marriage, both personally *and* professionally.

His lips pressed tight, and his brows furrowed. He studied her for a moment before answering. "I have absolute confidence in your ability to competently select the site of The Lion's Den Chicago club."

Brianna beamed a smile at him, sensing his sincerity.

"I can work out of my suite the next two days while you meet with the Realtor. I'm not here to micromanage you." Leopold paused a beat. "I missed you, so I rearranged my schedule."

She nodded as relief flooded her. He'd missed her? Should she admit she'd missed him too? He kept her out of sorts. Unsettled. She was never sure which way was up with him. It was worrisome and exciting at the same time.

"When was the last time you had an in-room massage?" Leopold asked with a quirked brow.

"Never." Brianna had never had an in-room massage. She hadn't had a massage in years; she'd been too busy running Parlora and Grayson's life for him.

Leopold let out a long, slow breath and shook his head. Was he angry? He turned to his left. "Please come in and set up."

She stepped aside as a middle-aged man and woman stepped into her room carrying portable massage tables and duffle bags. They moved the living room area furniture aside and unfolded their massage tables.

"This is Mr. and Mrs. Ivan and Alina Petrov. Our most sought-after massage therapists at the hotel. They've been kind enough to offer us their last appointment of the day." Leopold smiled at the couple and turned back to her.

"Thank you both. I've never had an in-room massage before." Brianna was stunned. Leopold's generosity and surprises amazed her. *Is this what he meant by taking care of his queen? But I'm not his queen. Not really.*

"We have vanilla-infused lavender scented oils and candles if that meets with your approval." Alina stated in a thick Russian accent.

It sounded heavenly. "That's perfect."

Leopold gestured to the bathroom. He began undressing after he closed the door behind them. Her pulse beat wildly as bit by bit, he exposed the strong muscles of his over six-foot five frame. She'd never tire of looking at him, with or without clothes on.

"You can't get a massage with your clothes on," he said as he shed the last of his clothing and donned the white hotel robe.

Her face heated. She'd been busted ogling him. She giggled and quickly got undressed and into the other robe. She felt a sense of feminine pride and her ego soared when Leopold did some ogling himself.

"Before we go back into the living room area, I just wanted to thank you, on behalf of all the Palermo women for the wonderful gift baskets. Angel now sees herself as a sophisticated big girl with her own body lotion and lip balm." Brianna placed a tender kiss on his kissable lips.

His smile made Brianna's heart swell with an emotion she couldn't identify. Affection? Fondness? She wasn't sure and didn't want to delve too deeply to figure it out.

"I was happy to do it. It did my heart good to bring a smile to all of your faces." He led Brianna by the hand back to the living room. The lights had been dimmed, the subtle scent of lavender and vanilla drifted through the room, and slow rhythmic music played from a portable CD player.

Alina pulled back the white sheet from her massage table and turned around. Ivan did the same with his. She and Leopold disrobed. Brianna lay face down on Alina's table and Leopold on Ivan's.

Sometime later, Brianna was gently shaken awake. "Let me get you to bed. You fell asleep during your massage." Leopold whispered and lifted her off the massage table. With strong, purposeful strides he carried her to the bed and tucked her in. "I'll finish up with Ivan and Alina and join you in a minute."

Brianna's massage had been so relaxing it had put her to sleep? She wasn't surprised. Alina's hands had worked magic on her tight, stressed muscles, easing out all the kinks.

Before she knew it, she was jarred awake by Leopold's blaring cellphone alarm. Cocooned in his warm embrace, she was reluctant to let go when he turned to shut the alarm off. She'd slept like the dead. Dreamed in vivid color. About cuddly lions of all things.

Unable to resist his naked form, she slid a hand down his muscled torso until she reached his impressive erection, amazed at his thickness. His cock grew, straining toward her as she stroked his length.

Leopold placed his hand over hers, stopping her. "We have enough time for quick showers and breakfast before our meeting with the Realtor."

Reluctantly she disengaged and gazed down at him, propped up on her elbow. Hair mussed from sleep and sleepy eyed, he was still beautiful to look at.

"You're no fun, Leo." She gently brushed her lips against his and then got out of bed. She mourned the loss of his sturdy frame and body heat immediately.

"It's Leopold. I've already demonstrated how much fun I can be. I'll make it up to you each night we're here after we take care of business. You also know I'm a man of my word, don't you?"

Yes, she did, and she looked forward to the next two nights in Chicago.

Early Friday afternoon, Brianna found herself on a restricted tarmac at O'Hare International Airport strolling toward Leopold's private Boeing 727. Emboldened with his initials LVH underneath the windows, the aircraft was also part of his family's corporate fleet.

Never having flown private before, she felt an adrenaline rush and a lightness in her chest. She stopped and snapped a few photos of the plane with her cell phone. A giggle escaped her lips. She heard Leopold chuckle behind her.

"If you think the outside is impressive, wait until you see the inside. I had the interior completely renovated two years ago. Give me your phone, I'll take pictures of you at the top of the airstairs."

Grateful he wasn't making fun of her over her reaction to a plane, Brianna handed him her phone and all but skipped to the stairs located near the back of the plane. Once at the top, she waved at a smiling Leopold taking pictures of her. Feeling silly, and unable to contain her smile no matter how hard she tried, she struck some sexy poses for her photographer on the ground.

He quickly joined her and led her inside. *Wow.* She took her phone back and clicked away getting shots of the interior. The interior had no resemblance to a traditional commercial plane.

The typical rows of seats had been removed and replaced with large, cream-colored leather seats with Leopold's initials branded on the back. Flat screen televisions and lacquered topped oak wood tables were disbursed at various spots with seats behind them.

Leopold gestured to seats behind a table near the middle of the plane. She sank into a plush leather seat and buckled herself in. He joined her just as who she assumed was the pilot, similar in stature to Leopold wearing a uniform approached them from the front of the plane.

He extended his hand and shook hers. "Welcome, Brianna. It's a pleasure to finally meet you. I'm Hans Livingston, your pilot today. My brother Evan is the co-pilot. Our cousin Leanna, your cabin attendant." Of course, they were all Leopold's cousins. What an amazing family.

"Thank you. Pardon my giddiness, I've never flown private before." Her face heated.

"There's nothing to forgive. Alph– cousin has ensured his guests experience a comfortable flight on his plane." He turned to Leopold. "*Ee gaan binnenkort van start.* After we reach cruising altitude, make sure to show Brianna the rest of the plane." He winked and returned to the cockpit.

"Dutch, our native language. We'll be taking off soon," Leopold explained.

She nodded and snapped a few more photos from where they sat before turning her phone off. Brianna acknowledged as they prepared for take-off, the trip had been a resounding success. They'd selected not one, but two locations – one in Chicago proper on Hubbard Street and another in Schaumburg on Lake Street. Several other suburban locations were in possible contention as the Chicago Metropolitan area was large.

Brianna braced herself as they accelerated down the runway and then took off, heading back home. True to his word, Leopold had made their nights together not only fun, but passionate as well. A first for her on a business trip.

"Since we're expanding the club in cities where your hotels are located, we should cross promote between the sanctuaries slash foundation, clubs, and hotels. Maximize exposure for all three." It wouldn't be difficult to do, all three of his businesses working together.

Leopold nodded, seemingly in agreement. "It makes sense, good idea. I hate to think about it, but we should incorporate the Fallen Angel program in the hotels. You never know. I'll have Benjamin coordinate the arrangements between the sanctuary for the animals for our new Illinois club locations."

For that, she was grateful. Brianna found the hierarchical dynamic of Leopold's inner circle unique. All were family members. Cousins. Benjamin appeared to be his second in command, and hers as well. Owen and Daniel offered support between Leopold and the rest of the family. Most importantly, all were devoted and loyal to him, without question.

Leopold unbuckled as soon as the Fasten Seat Belt sign turned off. She undid hers and accepted his offered hand.

He gestured toward the front and back of the plane. "With the different seating configurations, we have a thirty-one-passenger capacity. Two cabin crew seats. Multiple flat screen televisions and DVD players."

He led her to the spacious galley which

boasted shiny granite counter tops. A gorgeous, tall, blonde woman in a uniform similar to Hans's smiled warmly and extended her hand. Brianna shook it happily. She assumed it was Leanna, their cabin attendant.

"Welcome, Brianna. So wonderful to meet you at last. We've all heard great things."

They had?

"The family text thread is vast and wide, I'm afraid." Leopold chuckled and kissed his cousin on the cheek.

Leanna shrugged with a gleam in her eyes. "We have filet mignon, herb roasted fingerling potatoes, and bacon wrapped asparagus whenever you're ready." She announced.

Brianna's mouth nearly watered it sounded so delicious.

"Thank you. We should be ready to eat shortly. Let me finish showing Brianna around first."

The plane's renovations included new carpeting throughout, fresh paint, wi-fi system, two updated passenger lavatories, a guest bedroom with two twin beds and two passenger seats and a master with a king size bed, shower, bathroom, and passenger seats.

Leopold gestured to the bed in the master.

Something wrapped in a bright red bow rested on the center of it.

"For me?" Brianna sat down next to the gift and looked back at Leopold standing in the bedroom doorway. He'd been beyond generous already, and now another gift?

"Go on, open it. It's just a little something."

She swallowed a laugh, spirits high, and removed the bow from a beautiful heart-shaped crystal trinket box with frosted and smooth roses on it. Something appeared to be inside. A giggle escaped. The trinket box was filled with Hershey Kisses. Brianna unwrapped one and popped it in her mouth, savoring the chocolaty goodness of her favorite treat.

Leopold sat down next to her on the bed. "There's a card."

It was nestled in between the candies. She plucked it out of the box. *Let me kiss you now, so I can taste the flavors of your sweetness.*

His little gift was incredibly thoughtful. She wasn't used to such attention. Brianna trapped her lower lip between her teeth. She wasn't sure what to make of it all, but she knew she enjoyed being the object of his attention. Maybe *too* much.

Leopold flashed her a tempting, lethal smile. Following the card's directive, Brianna kissed him with a wildness she'd never known or allowed herself to experience before. She drank in the power of his kisses, his lips tasting like heaven and sweet, sinful delight.

Brianna felt the confident magnetism that for some reason she was nearly unable to resist. They tore at each other's clothing, a sensuous light passing between them.

When they were gloriously naked, Leopold scooted up on the bed and sat up with his back against the headboard, bringing her along with him. Brianna eagerly straddled his lap, brushing up against his thick cock.

She wrapped her slender hand around his thick stalk, and he grew even harder. Her hand moved in a steady rhythm eliciting a shudder and moans from his lips.

Leopold pulled her head toward him, and their mouths collided in a desperate, greedy kiss. Brianna felt her entire world tilt in a way it never had before. She rocked against the finger he slipped inside her wet channel, anticipating more. He rubbed her clit with deft fingers until she leaned her head back and cried out as convulsive waves gripped her.

"Ride my dick. I can't wait any longer," Leopold murmured, his plea urgent.

Brianna rose onto her knees and positioned his cock at her entrance. She looked down at

Leopold, his eyes had turned to liquid heat, and lust spiked through her veins.

She slowly lowered herself, capturing him, his thickness stretching her until she fully enveloped him. "Too big," she whispered. Nearly to the point of erotic pain.

Leopold lifted her up and eased her back down on his erection. She felt her insides quiver and burn.

"No, I'm not. You were made for me. *Only* me. Fuck me. *Hard*. Stop making me wait."

His sexy demand sent heat flashing through her. She rode him in earnest, sliding back and forth over his rigid, steely length. Hunger and challenge simmered between them, and she fucked him hard, as he'd asked her to.

Their eyes locked, and their breathing came in unison. He reached between their bodies and rubbed the little bundle of nerves making her insides tremble. Brianna squeezed her eyes closed, her body sizzling in an all-consuming heat. She groaned in ecstasy as Leopold gripped her hips, grunted, and filled her pussy with his warm cum.

They remained still for a moment. Her heart hammered against her ribs. Sparks continued dancing in the space around them. She was struck by the intensity of their connection. The feeling foreign to her.

Leopold wrapped a finger around tendrils of her curls. "You're so beautiful," he said with decisiveness.

Brianna shook her head. A tear rolled down her cheek and she closed her eyes.

"Look at me."

She opened her eyes and saw flickers of fierceness and possessiveness in his.

"You're beautiful here." He gently stroked her forehead and along her temple. "You're beautiful here." He trailed his finger along her chest where her heart was. "You're beautiful here." He tweaked her nipple, causing it to pebble from his warm touch. "And here." He tangled his fingers through her wavy locks. "You're beautiful inside and out. Don't ever doubt it."

Brianna nodded and brushed her lips against his. Her tummy growled, ruining the moment.

Leopold smiled up at her, his gaze warm and steady. "Maybe we should clean up and eat."

She'd rather stay in bed. She glanced at the trinket box filled with chocolate on the bedside table. "You don't think we can survive on sex and chocolate?"

He raised a brow with a seductive look in his

eyes. "And let the filet mignon go to waste after Leanna worked so hard preparing it for us?"

Her stomach growled again. She'd forgotten about the meal that was waiting on them. "I suppose you're right," she conceded.

"Why don't we test your sex and chocolate theory this weekend?" he suggested with a gleam in his eyes.

"Deal."

Chapter Eight

L eopold scanned the kitchen at The Lion's Den Manhattan Saturday morning shortly before Brianna's family, the children, and their families were due to arrive. He needed everything to be perfect for his mate. Anything less wasn't acceptable.

He stole a glance at Brianna. She was chatting with the chef and his minions while she sampled the food that was being offered for lunch. She ate a spoonful of four-cheese macaroni and cheese and moaned in delight.

His cocked stirred in his pants. He'd elicited many moans from his lovely mate last night after returning home from their Chicago business trip. They'd tested her sex and chocolate theory and had inevitably failed. But not before four rounds with his forever and too many Hershey Kisses to count. They'd satisfied their hunger with Chinese takeout before falling asleep with Prissy purring contently at the foot of the bed. It had been a perfect evening.

She carried her plate over to him. "Try this chicken tender. It's crispy on the outside and moist and flavorful on the inside."

He took a small bite; chicken tenders weren't usually on his menu. They were surprisingly tasty. The kids would love them. He tried a small piece of perfectly seasoned roast beef. Relief rushed through him. The chef had everything well in hand for lunch.

"Chef, this lunch buffet you've put together got me thinking. What if we offered our club loyalty program members a monthly or twice monthly Sunday brunch at all of our locations? You can change up the menu each time. It would give everyone an opportunity to prepare something other than the usual hot appetizers the club normally offers." Brianna's face lit up when the chef nodded enthusiastically.

"I love that idea. I can safely speak for the chefs at the other locations that we'd like the opportunity to do more in the kitchen than we're doing now." The chef eyed Leopold tentatively.

"You heard the boss. Work with Brianna and

the other chefs on the frequency of brunch, menu ideas, and the price."

The chef nodded triumphantly and led Brianna deeper into the kitchen, speaking excitedly about his ideas. With everything under control in the kitchen, Leopold excused himself and proceeded to the "animal room."

The scent of hay and straw tickled his nose. A requirement for inspectors, the room was only for show. The animals weren't "wild," lent from his sanctuary. They were shifters, but the inspectors didn't know that.

Benjamin, Oliver, and Daniel entered the room. He'd arranged for a lion, Siberian tiger, and Bengal white tiger at the children's request. As expected, the shifters were right on time.

"Hey, hey everyone! Is there room for one more?"

He turned and found his super-model cousin Mariska Baeten in the room's doorway. What was *she* doing here?

She entered and hugged him tight. "I'm in town for a few days before I have to be in London. I thought I'd lend a paw and also meet the alpha's mate. Has she consented yet?" Her hopeful expression made his gut clench.

"No, she hasn't. And she doesn't know about us yet either." He didn't actually mind. He wasn't going to rush Brianna, regardless of the threats made against him. Fuck the elders and their bullshit.

Mariska nodded, worry in her eyes. "Sire, I want you to know, if the worst comes to pass, rest assured, I'm with you. You have my undying loyalty. Always." Her eyes glistened with unshed tears. Benjamin, Owen, and Daniel nodded their agreement.

Leopold blew out a frustrated breath. He despised the elders for putting his pride in such an untenable situation. "Thank you all. And thank you for indulging me today for my mate's family. You don't normally go on display wearing leashes."

"We're happy to, Your Grace. The kids will have a great time and the afternoon will please our future queen," Benjamin said.

Pleasing his mate and her family was paramount to his own happiness, something he'd never thought would be the case. But there it was.

Leopold greeted Brianna's family, including her father, Aldo. Vito had driven him to the club. Four five-year-old little girls including Brianna's niece Angel and four ten-year-old boys including her nephew Matt couldn't contain their excitement. Their parents on the other hand, all wore the same concerned expressions on their faces.

Brianna joined him after everyone had settled in the main seating area of the club. "Is everyone excited about meeting the lions and tigers today?" Brianna asked, excitement in her voice.

"Yay!" the children shouted in unison.

"Good, I'm glad. I hate to be a chicken, but I'm going to watch from the bar area with Leo's mom."

"Is Leepold," Aldo corrected.

Brianna smirked at him and shrugged. "I know." She rushed over to the bar where his mother sat sipping white wine.

"Looks like Brianna will miss out on all the fun. I promised Angel and Matt lions and tigers for all of you today, and I always keep my promises. In fact, I've added a lady lion, or lioness to the group today." The children's eyes lit up and the parents stiffened.

"I assure you, there is nothing to be afraid of. The animals are specially trained. Gentle. Not like the animals you'd find in a typical zoo. They'll be brought out on leashes by handlers from my feline sanctuary. The handlers have tranquilizer guns with them as a precaution." The parents nodded, seemingly assured. "Feel free to take pictures with your phones, but I'll also have someone taking pictures. We'll post them online for everyone."

He turned around for a glance of his mate. She saluted him with her own glass of white wine. His mother winked. Leopold nodded at them both.

"Bring out the big cats please." He bellowed out for dramatic effect.

Benjamin roared as he was led in. The children squealed in delight. Their parents clutched their babies close to them. The senior handler positioned him beside Leopold.

"This is Benjamin. King of the jungle."

The children all clapped. Benjamin bowed his head. The parents appeared stunned, and Leopold hoped they would see there was nothing to fear as they were perfectly safe.

A low, menacing growl resounded in the club. Oliver strolled in with his handler like he owned the place. His guests took pause. Oliver took his place beside Benjamin.

"Meet Oliver, a Siberian tiger." Oliver raised his right front paw as if waving to everyone. The children giggled and waved back at him.

Everyone turned when Daniel chuffed as he entered the room with his handler and took his place beside Oliver. "This is Daniel, a white Bengal tiger."

"Beautiful," one of the parents said. "This is amazing. Thank you for inviting us today."

"You're more than welcome. But we're not finished with our introductions. Lastly, please welcome the lovely lioness Mariska."

His super-model cousin waltzed into the room as if she were on a runway – regal and sophisticated – for a feline. To Vito's dismay, Aldo reached out and pet her head gently, smiling from ear to ear.

"Dad, be careful," Vito warned.

Aldo chuckled, ignoring his son, and continued petting Mariska. The children watched in awe but refrained from touching the animals themselves. Everyone gasped when Mariska licked Aldo's face. Leopold felt his mate's anxiety behind him.

"It's okay children. She just kissing me. Right, Leepold?"

"Absolutely. She's a very friendly girl. As most of you know, I founded the LVH Feline Sanctuary and Foundation. We have roughly fifteen-acre sanctuaries in New York, Chicago, San Diego, and Phoenix that are home to about forty various jungle cats including lions, tigers, leopards, cheetahs and so on. We have a forty-five-hundred-acre sanctuary in Africa, about ninety minutes from Johannesburg."

One of the children's fathers nodded and frowned. "I've heard about some of the horrendous things that happen to these animals. What you're doing to try to help is extraordinary." Adults and children alike nodded enthusiastically.

Gratitude warmed his heart. He was pleased his audience was receptive to his foundation's work.

"Thank you. We're saving these beautiful animals from trophy or canned hunting operations, bone trade poaching, cub petting and breeding farms and human and animal conflicts. A year ago, we saved a badly injured pregnant cheetah. Her name is Sasha. She was so badly hurt, she ended up losing an eye, and two of her female cubs."

The little girls teared up. It was heartbreaking, he knew. "But her male cub survived. We named him George. Although she was badly hurt, she was a wonderful mommy to little George. He grew up big and strong and Sasha is fully recovered from her injuries, she lives at our New York sanctuary."

Angel raised her hand. "But what happened to George?"

"Yeah, where's George?" Matt asked.

The kids voiced their dismay over George's whereabouts.

"Don't worry. George is fine. We rotate the

animals between the sanctuaries to change up their environments, stimulate their senses and to keep them from getting bored so they live a happy life. The African sanctuary has sixteen different enclosures we can transfer the animals to." He turned to Benjamin's trainer. "Where is George right now?"

"The San Diego sanctuary. Sasha didn't respond well to being transferred. I believe she grew attached to all of us in New York since we saved her and she feels safest here, so New York is her permanent home. Eventually George will transfer back so they'll be able to spend time together."

The trainer's explanation brought smiles to the children and parents faces alike. His lion enjoyed spending time with Sasha playing at the sanctuary. He related to her as a sibling of sorts.

"How about we talk a little bit about lion's and tiger's characteristics and traits and then you can pet them and take pictures?"

Nods from all his guests was encouraging.

"Let's begin with our beautiful lioness." Mariska softly roared for their guests, as the practiced performer she was.

"Lions are the only cat species to live in social groups called prides. Female lions are bold and fierce as the pride's primary hunters. They're also gentle and nurturing as they care for the babies, or cubs." The mothers nodded, smiling at each other. The fathers clasped their hands together, blinking rapidly.

Leopold pet Benjamin's head and ran his fingers through his mane. Although his beta's mane was impressive, *his* was even more so. He was the alpha after all. The king of his jungle.

"The male lions defend the pride's territory. They'll watch the cubs while the lionesses are hunting. You can tell them apart from the females by their thick manes. Scientists don't know why lions are the only big cats that can grow a mane."

Matt raised his hand. Leopold nodded.

"They can lose their manes though, right?" The boy knew that?

Everyone's eyes widened.

"Yes. It's true. If a male lion is badly hurt, or overly stressed, they can lose it. Once they're well again, it will grow back. It can take up to a year." Leopold had witnessed it firsthand, with a male lion shifter in his pride. Served the fucker right.

"The male lion in charge is referred to as the alpha. He runs the show and everyone in the pride respects his authority." Benjamin gave him the stink eye and nudged him. Oliver and Daniel rolled their eyes. Mariska ignored him completely and yawned.

Amused but undeterred, Leopold continued. "The alpha's second in command is his beta. He helps the alpha with his duties. The omega is the peacekeeper of the pride. And the delta works very hard supporting the pride." Although he was describing a wild lion's pride in broad strokes, as he glanced at Benjamin, Oliver, and Daniel he was describing how they all interacted. They not only were his family, but they were his closest friends and indispensable to him and their pride. It made his blood boil to know that everyone under his leadership was now in jeopardy because of the elders.

"Lions are the only cat species with a tufted tail tip," Matt shared.

True. "A lion cub's tail won't get that tuft until they're two or three months old. A lion's tail is very muscular."

Benjamin's tail whipped around and swiped Leopold in the face. Smart ass. The children found his beta's antic hysterical.

"Lions actually walk on their toes, not their feet." Matt offered. The little boy was a wealth of information.

Leopold nodded. "Yes, that's true. They like the scent of citronella and catnip. It makes them feel happy, like it does for your pet cats. And lion fossils have been found that are over two million years old." He was proud of the animal side of his nature.

He was curious about Matt, however. Leopold moved to stand between Oliver and Daniel. He rubbed the tops of their heads. "Matt, do you know anything about tigers?"

Matt smiled wide and nodded. "Yup. They're the biggest of the big cats. The tiger's stripes are unique, like our fingerprints. If you shave their fur, you'll see their skin has stripes too. The girl tigers can have up to five babies at a time. They love to swim and play in the water. They usually hunt alone at night and can live to twenty-five." His eyes lit with pride when everyone applauded.

"How do you know so much about big cats, young man?" The senior handler asked.

Matt sat up tall in his seat. "I've been studying. I want to be a zoologist one day."

Matt's friends looked confused. "What's a zoologist?" one finally asked.

Matt glanced at Leopold, seemingly asking for permission to answer. Leopold nodded.

"They study animal behavior and how animals act in the wild. They do research projects and write articles for science magazines. They collect and study animal information. And they help with animal conservation, like Leopold does." Matt nodded, appearing satisfied with his explanation.

For a ten-year-old, the explanation was perfect. Leopold's nose twitched when he scented Kaylee. In her leopard form. What the fuck was she doing there? His lion growled. The four animals on display all turned, having obviously scented her as well.

"Oh cool! A black panther," one of the boys called out, pointing at Kaylee. A chorus of oohs and aahs filled the room.

Leopold held out his hand. "Tranquilizer gun." The nearest handler placed it in his hand. At that moment he wished it were an actual gun.

In horror, he watched Kaylee prowl toward Brianna. His mate's eyes widened in apparent terror, and she trembled. His mother stepped in front of Brianna in an effort to block Kaylee's access to her. Although it was soft, with is sensitive shifter hearing, he heard Kaylee hiss and growl. The fucking bitch. How *dare* she? He unbuckled his belt and pulled it free from the belt loops.

"Kaylee!" The defiant feline turned her attention to her alpha. Her hisses and growls immediately changed to the typical sawing like sounds leopards made, as if it would make a difference to him. "Come here. *Now*."

Kaylee sauntered to him as if she didn't have a care in the world, although now silent. When she reached Leopold, she sat and looked up at him innocently. Sensing Brianna had calmed down eased his fury but only slightly. He knelt in front of her, slipped his belt around Kaylee's neck, and secured it. She was lucky he hadn't choked her with it.

"Kaylee is a black leopard, not a panther. It looks like she wanted to join the party." Everyone laughed. He was grateful they hadn't noticed anything was wrong.

"Matt, want to share what you know about leopards with everyone?" Leopold was so angry he shook with it. He needed a moment to regain his bearings before rejoining his guests.

"Sure! Leopards are really fast. They can run up to thirty-six miles an hour. They like to climb trees and sometimes they'll drag their food up in a tree so no other animals will steal it. They can hear five times more sounds than people can. They're real strong swimmers. Because their spots look like roses, sometimes they're called rosettes. Like tigers, a leopard's spots are unique only to them."

For everyone's benefit, he stroked Kaylee lovingly, hating every minute of it. "One wrong move on your part and I'll snap your fucking neck. I don't give a shit who witnesses it. You hear me?" He whispered. Kaylee rubbed her head against Leopold's chest and his stomach churned. God, he hated her.

He stood and led Kaylee to his guests. They all appeared intrigued, not afraid. "Very good Matt, thank you. See? She's not completely black. If you look closely, you can see her spots or rosettes." Everyone nodded as they looked Kaylee over and she basked in the attention she didn't deserve.

"Would everyone be interested in a private visit to the New York sanctuary in the next few weeks?" Leopold would arrange for Matt to shadow the handlers and zoologists at the facility. He was a good kid and Leopold was interested to see how Matt would respond in the environment he claimed he wanted to work in when he was older.

A resounding agreement from his guests clinched the deal. They began checking their calendars to set a date. Leopold directed parents who wanted to donate to his foundation to Brianna so she could process their payments and enter them in the September charity gala drawing.

Holding on tightly to the belt leash he'd secured on Kaylee and with the tranquilizer gun firmly in his hand, the kids and adults enjoyed themselves petting and talking to the animals. Matt held court sharing other feline factoids. He was pleased his mate's family were getting into the spirit of the visit. Vito watched over Brianna's father like a hawk, but Aldo made sure to spend a little time with each animal.

When it appeared everyone had taken all the pictures they'd wanted to and had spent ample time with each animal, Leopold decided to conclude the interaction portion of their visit.

"All right everyone, the animals need to get back to the sanctuary now. It's feeding time for them as well as us." Leopold's heart swelled when final hugs and pets were given before the handlers led his family away. They'd been great sports. He knelt in front of Kaylee and whispered in her ear. "Rest assured, we're going to have a conversation about your behavior today. Get dressed and go home." He righted himself and handed the senior handler Kaylee's belt leash and the tranquilizer gun. He breathed a sigh of relief when Kaylee was out of sight.

Brianna joined him immediately after the animals had left the room. Her delectable lips curved into a warm smile. Leopold had pleased her. His lion roared with joy.

"I trust you all had a great time with the

animals? How about a round of applause for your gracious host?" Brianna placed her hand on his shoulder while his guests cheered him on.

Leopold felt his face heat. He'd do anything for his mate. Their little get together was nothing. "Thank you. It was my pleasure." He retrieved the list with everything on the lunch buffet menu from his pocket. "I've had a sampling, so I know you'll also enjoy the lunch buffet. For the children we have bagel dogs, mini cheeseburger sliders, mini pizzas, chicken fingers, macaroni and cheese, and french fries."

"That sounds good to me," one of the fathers said.

After the laughter died down, Leopold continued. "In addition, for the adults we have fried chicken, slow roasted roast beef, mashed potatoes, gravy, and a salad bar. We have different flavored cupcakes for dessert. We don't open for business until three o'clock so take your time and enjoy. The bar is open for the adults with milk, juice, and soft drinks for the children."

Leopold clapped along with his happy guests and watched everyone disburse to get their food and drinks. Not surprisingly, Angel and Matt opted to sit with their friends, leaving him with Brianna's adult family members.

After they'd all filled their plates and sat

down to eat, Brianna's family all thanked him, excitedly talking over each other. Leopold and his lion felt ten feet tall.

He chuckled at their enthusiasm, although thanks weren't necessary. They ate in companiable silence for a moment. The chef and his staff had outdone themselves. Everything was delicious and he was certain their Sunday brunch idea would be a huge success.

"I was thinking. I visit the South African sanctuary at least twice a year. I'd like to take all of you there. So you can experience the extent of what my foundation is trying to do. It would be an excellent educational experience for Matt."

Their mouths fell open in surprise. Their smiles told him they liked the idea.

"Um, Leo, that's a generous offer, but I'm not sure it's a good idea." Brianna's frown broke his heart. Her doubts about him hurt, even though he didn't blame her. She'd been through a lot with her asshole ex-husband.

"Brianna, is Leepold," Aldo corrected.

She pinched the bridge of her nose and sighed. "I know, Dad."

His mother smiled at him and nodded from her seat among their guests. "You don't have to worry. Regardless of what may happen with your job, or us, I'd like for us to take this trip together.

It's something important to me I want to share with all of you. You have my word I won't change my mind and you know I'm a man of my word."

A pretty blush stained her cheeks. He absolutely adored his mate. How had he gotten so lucky?

"I say we should go." Aldo began. "Is a trip of a lifetime, not only for Matteo, but for all of us."

His future father-in-law was right of course. Leopold wanted to share many lifetime experiences with them.

Brianna remained silent but nodded, apparently conceding.

"It's going to be a nightmare booking flights for everyone though," Jilly said while she rocked baby DJ in her arms.

Brianna rolled her eyes and scoffed. "No, it won't. Mr. Boss Man has his own 727. There's plenty of room for all of us and then some."

Chapter Nine

Brianna snuck into her office when the last of the club's guests and her family had left. Matt was barely able to contain his excitement for their upcoming New York sanctuary visit and 'African adventure' as he'd referred to it.

She was overwhelmed by Leopold's generosity that now extended to her family. She was more concerned that she was falling hard for the man and couldn't seem to help herself. She enjoyed being with him, was drawn to him, and that terrified the hell out of her. Brianna was petrified to take a chance on Leopold even with all the kindness, respect, and consideration he'd shown her. She hated her ex-husband for messing with her head so badly she was too afraid to give another relationship, a potentially amazing relationship, a try.

She noticed a note on her laptop keyboard as she sat down behind her desk. *Your voice and laughter were my favorite things until I heard you moan.* Her entire body warmed recalling how Leopold had made her moan the night before after they'd returned from Chicago. They'd enjoyed Chinese food after failing to sustain themselves with Hershey Kisses and sex.

When Prissy had jumped onto the foot of the bed as they'd settled in to sleep, Brianna hadn't flinched. She had Leopold to thank for helping her get over her fear of cats. She kept her collection of Leopold's notes in a keepsake box with trinkets and pictures from when her mother was alive.

Brianna took stock of the nearly perfect afternoon. The creepy interaction with the black leopard named Kaylee, of all names, had shaken her. She'd felt like a fool when Leopold's mother had stepped in front of her, shielding her from the hissing and growling big cat. The menacing looks directed at her from the leopard had reminded Brianna of the dirty looks she'd received from her human employee Kaylee. It had been bizarre to say the least. Fortunately, Kaylee the leopard appeared to be fond of

Leopold and had been well behaved after he'd called to her.

Thinking back on how the children had been fearless in their interaction with the tame, gentle animals earlier, Brianna felt silly. After the minor incident with leopard Kaylee, she should have joined everyone and pet the animals. Her father had spent time with each animal and had her brother Vito take pictures. If he and the children could be brave, so could she. She decided then and there on the following Tuesday, she'd stay after hours and meet the animals brought to the club.

When Chloe and Leopold entered her office, she shut down her laptop and tucked Leopold's little love note into her purse. She rounded her desk and gave Chloe a quick hug.

"We missed you today." Brianna commented.

Chloe wrapped an arm around Brianna's waist and embraced her. "I'm sorry. Mason's folks are in town for the weekend, so we spent some time with them. I heard it was a great afternoon though."

It had been, minor issues aside. "You heard right. Did you also hear your brother invited my family to the African sanctuary? I'd love it if you joined us. Sometime after the charity gala."

Chloe's eyes lit up. "Count me in. I haven't visited for two years."

Brianna approached Leopold and held him tight. Flames spread through her body and her pulse sped up as it always did whenever they touched. "Thank you for everything today. The kids and their parents were thrilled. Matt is over the moon about shadowing the handlers and zoologists during our New York sanctuary visit. And don't get me started about the African trip."

Leopold kissed her forehead, his lips warm and soft. "It was my pleasure. I'm sorry about how Kaylee acted. She was an unexpected and unwelcomed guest."

The experience with the black leopard had been bizarre. But how did a leopard end up at the club without a handler as an unexpected guest? And all the animal's names were the same as Leopold's family member's names. It had been a strange coincidence.

"Did you realize the animals had the same names as your cousins? Including Mariska? And I don't know if I was just freaked out but that angry look the black leopard gave me before you called her over, reminded me a lot of Kaylee Hart." Brianna was probably making an issue out of something that didn't exist, but she wasn't one to not speak her mind.

Leopold and Chloe exchanged a knowing glance. Perhaps there was an issue. Brianna couldn't imagine what it might be.

Leopold nodded. "The animals everyone met today are my cousins and Kaylee Hart. Our family are animal shifters. Benjamin, Oliver, Daniel, Mariska, and Kaylee weren't borrowed from the sanctuary. They'd shifted from their human forms into their animal forms."

What? Had she heard him correctly? He had to be joking. Since they'd started spending time together, she'd gotten Leopold to loosen up a little. He had to be pulling her leg. Animal shifters were something from movies and books. They didn't exist in real life.

Brianna backed away from Leopold and Chloe, unsure of what to make of them and everything she'd experienced earlier. "That's not possible. You said so yourself, the sanctuary animals were specially trained to be friendly."

Chloe stopped Leopold from approaching her. Brianna appreciated Chloe's understanding.

"It's true. All the families can shift into animals. Mostly lions, but also tigers, leopards, cougars, and other felines." Chloe tried to explain.

Brianna shook her head. It wasn't possible. They had to be crazy. That's what super wealth could do to a person, and the Van Housen clan had shitloads of money. More than most people could fathom. Brianna looked over to Leopold. The intensity of his stare pierced through her.

"Leopold is our leader. Our alpha. Our king. He leads our pride and oversees Van Housen Corp. And he's the president of the North American Shifter Collective and leads the United States faction. Our family founded the International Shifter Syndicate," Chloe said matter-of-factly.

Brianna scoffed. "Bullshit. Are those some sort of rich people cult organizations or something?"

The disappointment on Chloe's face made Brianna almost regret what she'd just said. It was all insane, Chloe had to know that. Brianna stepped back a little more, adding more distance between her, Chloe, and Leopold.

Chloe shrugged. "Show her, big brother."

Show her? What the hell did Chloe mean by that? Brianna turned her gaze on Leopold, and he got down on all fours. Before her eyes, his skin sprouted golden fur, she heard bones crack and he morphed into an enormous lion.

"*Jesus Christ*. What the fuck is happening?" Brianna drew in a stuttered gasp. A scream sliced through the fog in her brain. She stepped back until the backs of her legs met with the office's leather couch. Tears sprung to her eyes and slid down her cheeks. Chloe rushed to her side and gently helped her sit down.

"Don't cry, sweetie. It's just Leopold. Our king. As his lion. Everything is fine." Chloe embraced her tightly, softly rocking her.

Brianna sniggered. "Sure. Everything's just fine. People can turn into animals. Just another day in Manhattan, right? How is this possible? Why doesn't everyone know about this?" She stammered.

"We've been careful to stay under the radar. That's why we founded the International Shifter Syndicate. To keep us safe." She met Brianna's gaze, seeming to will her to understand. The shifter revelation was surreal. She turned when Leopold the lion advanced toward them slightly, then stopped.

But as Brianna thought about it calmly for a moment, she believed she understood. Knowing the world and people as she did, these shifter-humans would most likely be hunted down and tortured, experimented on or killed. Then she thought of her brother Vito, the former marine. She'd bet the military would want to use the shifters as weapons of some kind.

Wait...we? Brianna looked Chloe over. She appeared like everyone else. As Leopold did and the rest of his family did. And their Uncle

Hendrick, the four-star general. "You're a lioness?"

Chloe slipped her hand inside Brianna's and squeezed lightly. "I'm a snow leopard. Mariana and Willem adopted me. Leopold found when I was twelve-years-old when my first adoptive parents kicked me out of the house after I shifted for the first time. It was a crazy, scary time. I had no idea I was a shifter, but rather than try and help me, they were afraid and threw me out. Leopold literally saved my life."

Brianna's heart ached for her friend. She couldn't even imagine what it must have been like for her as a young girl learning she could become an animal. Chloe was an amazing woman. One Brianna was happy to call her friend.

"It's all right, hon. Ancient history we can talk about another time. Want to meet Leopold in lion form?" Chloe waved the lion over.

Did she? Brianna stiffened for a moment. As a lion, Leopold was larger than Benjamin was and had a regal air about him. Chloe had referred to him as their king. That explained the jeweled crown Brianna had seen in his office placed on top of a red velvet pillow. She'd noticed a tiny version of his crown at his house on one of the fireplace mantels. She hadn't said anything about it, but now she suspected it belonged to Prissy. Matching crowns. She could admit that was actually cute.

The lion slowly advanced toward them. Brianna was fearful yet fascinated. When he reached them, he sat on his hind legs and tilted his head up. His thick mane on full display. Was he peacocking? Brianna let a giggle escape.

Chloe stroked Leopold's head. "You have to forgive him. The male lions and their manes. They're worse than women."

Brianna touched Leopold's head where Chloe's hand had just been. Soft and warm. "Did he tell you my niece accidentally got gum in his hair when he came with me to Sunday dinner?"

Chloe's eyes widened. "Oh no. *That* must have been interesting."

Leopold grunted but remained still.

Brianna stroked Leopold's impressive mane. "Does he understand us?"

He grunted and nodded his head.

Brianna chuckled, slid off the couch, and hugged Leopold around the neck, burying her face in his fluffy mane. *Unbelievable.* She was amazed at the ease she felt, considering.

"Of course. In shifter form, we're still us. We understand humans. We can't respond with words obviously." Chloe answered.

Nothing was obvious to Brianna at the moment. She frowned when she noticed the scars on the bridge of Leopold's nose. She kissed the scars. What could have caused them? He was perfect, beautiful and strong in every other way. Brianna was astonished at her odd attraction to his lion form.

"Ten years ago, when Willem passed on the alpha and family business responsibilities to Leopold, he was challenged by another member of our pride that had issue with a hybrid taking over," Chloe said.

"Hybrid?"

"Willem is a shifter. Both of his parents are shifters. Mariana is a human, so technically Leopold is considered a hybrid. Anyway, he won the challenge. He nearly killed his opponent but showed mercy because the challenger was a family member. His scars are from that battle. No one has made issue with his leadership since." Chloe stroked Leopold's nose.

Brianna wasn't sure what to say. These confessions were beyond belief.

"But everything's going to work out now. Since you and Leopold are fated mates and you know about us now." Chloe announced happily.

Brianna stopped petting Leopold and sat back down on the couch. Leopold made a sound similar to a moan, but she couldn't worry about that. Fated mates? Like she'd read in paranormal romance novels?

"What are you talking about?" It had to be something different than what Brianna thought it was.

"As shifters, we have a destined mate that's meant to be ours forever. It's an instinctual thing. When we meet our mate, our animal recognizes them right away. Leopold knew you were his mate the day you met. At the club when you interviewed for General Manager. Don't you feel the mating bond? The pull?"

Brianna's jaw fell open. Was *that* the attraction she felt toward him? Why she couldn't resist him regardless of what she told herself? It was all some strange animal thing she had no control over? She bolted off the couch, needing to get away.

"This is all too much, Chloe. It's crazy. I can't be Leopold's mate. I'm sorry."

Brianna rushed out of her office and raced down the stairs. She barely remembered the drive home, too distraught to think clearly. When she got to her condo, she bolted the door and leaned against it, her heart racing. *What the hell is going on?*

She jumped when her phone rang. Chastising

herself for hoping it might be Leopold, she dug it out of her purse. She stared at the unfamiliar number before deciding to connect the call.

"Finally! Thank you for picking up," Grayson said.

Brianna's stomach fisted. He was the *last* person she wanted to speak to. *Perfect timing as always, asshole.*

"Look Grayson, you've got to stop calling me. I'd rather not have to, but I'll change my number." Her emotions swirled as she wrestled with her anger and frustration toward him.

"You don't need to do that. Just listen for a minute. *Please.*"

She wrapped herself in the blanket her mother had given her when she'd first become sick and paced the living room as Grayson rambled on about how they were perfect for each other. How they had a long history together, all the way back to college and to not be hasty and throw it all away. He begged her to return to California so they could pick up where they'd left off. He'd made some mistakes, but he'd changed. She could help him expand Parlora like they'd planned before she'd cut and run, leaving him in the lurch.

Brianna stopped in her tracks. Was he fucking serious? She seethed, tension gnawing at her insides. Going back to California and Grayson would be the easy way out. The familiar compared to what she was going through at the moment. But she'd be going back to a lying, cheating asshole who wanted to use her for her business acumen, while not valuing, respecting, or supporting her. Fuck that *and* him.

Leopold came to mind. Even before today's revelations, he'd been the opposite of Grayson in every way that mattered to her.

Taking the easy way out wasn't easy at all. She might be uncertain about many things, but she was certain about Grayson.

"Listen closely, because I'm not going to repeat myself again." Brianna would change her phone number immediately; Grayson had left her no choice. She'd see what her legal options were. She was through being harassed. "Leave me alone. Move on. We're over and that's never going to change. Have one of your girlfriends help you expand Parlora. Oh, that's right, they're all servers without an MBA. Good luck with that." She disconnected the call and shut her phone off. She wouldn't turn it back on until she had a new number.

"Are you alright? Can you let me in?" Chloe asked from the other side of Brianna's door. *Was* she alright? She would be. There was so much to process, but Brianna was confident she'd be fine in the long run.

Brianna opened the door and Chloe stepped inside. She hugged her bringing fresh tears to Brianna's eyes.

"It's going to be fine. You'll see. I didn't mean to freak you out back at the club. It's just that finding your mate is like a miracle. Some shifters never find theirs." Chloe's wistful expression was endearing. She was obviously a romantic.

"I don't know what to say. This is a lot to consider. You have to understand that." Brianna was human after all, and only just discovering animal shifters existed. Chloe needed to cut her some slack.

Chloe nodded. "I do, honest. But it's important that you accept and consent to Leopold being your mate. The International Shifter Syndicate elders threatened to remove him from his leadership positions if he didn't mate and make an effort to produce an heir by the time Leopold turns forty at the end of the year. Everything he's worked so hard for could be taken away. His legacy would be ruined. You can't let that happen."

Brianna's heart sank. Heirs? Legacy? Fate or whatever forces were at play had to be mistaken. She wasn't the one who could save him. She couldn't be his fated mate. She stopped short of suggesting Leopold fulfill the elders' demands with Kaylee as she clearly wanted Leopold. The thought made her stomach churn. What a mess.

Leopold shook his head in disappointment as he listened to the exchange between his mate and Chloe in the hallway on the other side of the closed door. He sensed Brianna's anguish and confusion as well as Chloe's sadness. He needed to remedy the situation somehow.

He knocked on the door and was grateful when Brianna allowed him inside. She had a blanket wrapped around her and her eyes were red and swollen from crying. As were Chloe's. Damn it.

"You didn't have to come all the way here. Chloe told me everything. I'm more certain than ever I can't be your mate. The fates or whatever instinctual thing you believe in has to be wrong. I can't help you with the elders' ultimatum. I can't consent to being your mate." Brianna's shoulders sagged, seeming defeated. Perhaps she didn't want to believe what she'd just said.

"Chloe shouldn't have said anything. It was wrong of her." Leopold knew his sister meant well, but she'd made the situation worse and upset his mate. That was unacceptable.

Tears streamed down Chloe's face. "I'm sorry, sire. I don't want you to lose everything you've work so hard for. I know it wasn't my place to tell Brianna, but I'm afraid for you."

Leopold understood, but it was too late now.

"Why not mate with Kaylee? She hates me anyway. Thinks I'm in the way and stole the General Manager position from her." Brianna's suggestion sounded weak to Leopold's and his lion's ears. She didn't mean it and he'd never consider it.

Chloe's face paled. He understood how she felt.

"Kaylee never meant anything to me. There was never much between us and after you and I met, there was nothing at all. She was merely a distraction until I found *you*." Did their mating bond assure Brianna he was being truthful?

Brianna's lips curved into a small smile.

"Chloe, please leave us. I need to speak with Brianna alone."

His sister nodded sadly and hugged his mate before hugging him. "I just love you both so much. I want you to be together. Happy." Chloe left without another word.

He shoved his hands in his pants pockets,

sighed, and shook his head. "It's true. I've worked very hard for many years for my family and those under my leadership. But for what? To make my family ultra-wealthy and then have them just pull the rug out from under me leaving me with a big house, a kitten, and fancy toys? What about *me*? What *I* want? I'm a billionaire in my own right. Maybe there was a subconscious reason I built up my own companies and pursued my own interests. Maybe I knew one day I might need to strike out on my own. Be independent from the rest of my family."

"Do you really believe that?" Brianna pulled her blanket more tightly around her.

Leopold nodded. "I do. The elders' threats are bullshit. Unfair and unreasonable. In a few months I'll know if they're real or some sort of game. But I honestly don't care anymore and I'm not going to pressure you into consenting to be my mate. I have faith you'll do it when you're ready."

Brianna shook her head sadly. "You don't understand. I'm not what you need or what the elders are demanding. I had a lot of trouble conceiving with Grayson and then when I finally did, I miscarried just after I passed my first trimester."

That explained the shared look between

Brianna and Jilly at Sunday dinner. They'd both experienced the trauma of losing a child. His heart ached for what she must have gone through. Especially having to go through it with an asshole like Grayson.

He didn't scent any health issues or illnesses from her, however. "I would never make light of your loss, but maybe you weren't meant to have children with him."

"I thought that too. Our relationship was such a trainwreck when I got pregnant."

"Whether or not we can eventually conceive doesn't matter to me. It's about more than the elders' threats. It's about my future. *Our* future. I'd like to help Lara and her friends open their salon in Manhattan, where they'll feel safe." He was relieved when he wrapped his arms around her and she didn't pull away.

"Why would you do that?" she asked as she snuggled against him.

"Because you're my family now and that means your family is mine too. Consider it an investment in *our* family's future. And don't worry, I employ an army of attorneys. I'll ensure everyone's interests are protected."

Brianna gazed up at him with uncertainty. "These expensive, grand gestures won't sway me to consent. I hope you know that. It's never been about the money for me."

Leopold kissed her forehead. "I know that, and it doesn't matter. I'm not going anywhere. I've been yours since the day we met, regardless of mating consent."

Brianna squeezed her eyes closed and a single tear escaped through her lashes. "You can't say things like that to me."

"You make my soul smile," he began, "Time stands still when I'm with you."

She shook her head, her eyes still closed.

"It's not just what I feel for you, it's what I don't want and will not feel for anyone else. Ever."

Leopold claimed her lips, their kiss was deep and all consuming. He held her close, so she felt his body's response to her.

"I never knew mates had a flavor until I tasted the sweetness of your lips on my tongue."

He led Brianna to her bedroom and eased her onto the bed. She gazed back at him, her eyes hazy with desire. Leopold removed his shirt and tossed it aside. "You are the rest of my life. I love you. It's alright that you're afraid and can't say it back yet. I can feel your love for me."

"The mating bond," Brianna said, sounding as if she believed. He hoped that was the case.

"Yes, mate. Our *forever* bond." He removed his pants and boxer briefs and hurled them toward his shirt.

Slowly, Leopold pulled Brianna's curve hugging black jeans and purple lacey panties off, eyeing his fill of her luscious form. The scent of her arousal drifted to his nose, and he felt his cock harden. His lion moaned. He lifted her arms up above her head and stripped off her purple Henley T-shirt and purple lace bra. Leopold ached at the sight of his mate spread out on the bed just for him. He was a lucky man. And lion.

He positioned himself on top of her, her soft warm skin against his. She wrapped her arms and legs around him, capturing him. He was a more than willing, eager captive. Smoldering flames danced in his mate's eyes.

Leopold traced her lower lip with his tongue, tasting her sweetness and then sucked that full lip into his mouth.

"Tell me where you want my lips to go and get lost in their journey." He whispered.

Brianna shivered beneath him, encouraging him.

His lips touched her nipple and gently bit down with tantalizing possessiveness. "Here?"

"Ye…yes," she whispered.

Leopold laved and suckled on Brianna's

pebbled peaks while she tangled her fingers through his hair. His lips traveled down her torso to her navel, dipping his tongue inside. "Here?"

"Yes," she confirmed. He nuzzled and licked in and around her navel and then continued on his journey toward the swell of her hips.

"Here?"

"Everywhere," she breathed.

A smile curved his lips. She was perfect, and she was his. Forever. He kissed and nibbled his way downward until he was nestled between her legs. The scent of her arousal set his heart on fire.

Leopold swiped his tongue along the length of her drenched slit. Brianna's thighs clenched around his head. He sheathed his tongue inside her tight pussy, and she tugged on his hair. He welcomed the sting.

She arched into him as he nipped, flicked, and teased her distended clit. He worked Brianna over, tormenting her sensitive flesh until she cried out her pleasure, her body vibrating in response to his sensual attention.

Leopold licked his lips, his mate tasted like ambrosia. Emboldened by his own reckless desire for her, he pushed her knees up and wedged himself between her thighs. His soul sang when Brianna grew bold and guided him inside her wet, snug pussy. His lion roared in ecstasy.

He drove in and out of her with sure strokes, her tight heat gripping him. He fucked her with the passion of his beast. Brianna lifted her hips meeting his thrusts. He stretched her, filling her with is thick dick. When he felt his spine tingle, he quickened his strokes, savoring her tight heat and rubbed her clit. A gasp escaped through her lips, and he groaned in response.

Leopold grasped Brianna's hips, pulling her hard into his final thrust. His pulsing cock filled her channel with hot ribbons of cum. She clung to him as she crashed over. He felt the pleasure ripple through her.

Leopold was semi-hard when he pulled out of her. He gathered Brianna against him, needing the feel of her silky skin against his. He knew for certain he'd never tire of his mate and looked forward to the years ahead of them.

He felt her body relax against his and sigh, he believed, in satisfaction.

"My love for you will never die. I'll love you the only way I know how – completely." Leopold assured Brianna. He felt her stiffen and held her close until she settled beside him.

"It would destroy me if you hurt me, Leo," Brianna whispered.

"It's Leopold, and I won't. I'll keep your heart safe, tucked inside my soul."

Chapter Ten

Two weeks later, Leopold observed his mate fussing over Matt like a mother hen, on their way to his New York feline sanctuary. They all wore casual clothes for the day ahead, with VIP badges hanging from red lanyards around their necks. His guests would receive the same badges when they arrived at the facility a bit later. The three of them were getting an earlier start to give Matt an opportunity to shadow sanctuary personnel and get a glimpse into what a career in zoology might be like.

Leopold had prepared them crispy bacon, egg, and cheese panini sandwiches and seasoned breakfast potatoes to eat on the way. Although the Chrysler 300 stretch limousine Leopold had chosen for their ride sat twelve and was obviously more than the three of them needed for the drive over, he'd wanted to give the boy an experience he'd never forget.

When the car had pulled up in front of Lara and Tommy's home, they and some of their neighbors had congregated around the car and taken pictures with a smiling Matt proudly posing in front of it. The boy had been gracious and had wanted a few shots with his little sister Angel beside him. He was a good kid.

She's going to be a wonderful mother one day. His lion agreed. Brianna engaged with Matt while they ate and watched some kid's show on the car's flat screen. Leopold didn't mean to diminish the anguish Brianna must have and still probably felt over losing her and Grayson's baby, but he also truly believed she was only meant to carry *his* children. Even if she was doubtful right now. Chloe had mentioned to him in confidence she'd be honored to be their surrogate if the need arose. He appreciated his sister's offer but didn't think it would be necessary when the time came.

They'd cleaned up with sanitizing wipes Brianna had in her purse, just as the car pulled up to the sanctuary's employee entrance. Matt was nearly bouncing in his seat.

"You excited there, buddy?" Leopold was excited for him. Such a simple gesture on his part, meant the world to the boy. He hoped Matt wouldn't be disappointed.

"Heck, yeah!" He grinned from ear to ear.

With Leopold holding Brianna's hand and Brianna holding Matt's, Leopold led them, like the family they were, to the first stop of their day. The cub feeding room.

Leopold had briefed Brianna on sanctuary operations. Most of the employees were shifter family and friends. Those who weren't, were allies of his family. Although handled and trained to a certain extent, the animals were wild. Of importance to him, everyone was looking forward to meeting her. His mate.

He guided Brianna and Matt inside the warm cub feeding room. A pet pen with soft blankets covering the bottom was nestled in the corner of the room. Two tiny guests of honor slept with pacifiers in their mouths, cuddled against each other and their respective lion and tiger stuffed animals. Leopold never tired of spending time with cubs. They were incredibly cute.

Matt craned his neck trying to see inside the pen.

His senior zoologist, a tiger shifter joined them. "I'm Josh, the sanctuary's senior zoologist.

Which one of you is Matteo Palermo? I'm told he's been studying because he wants my job." Josh winked at Leopold with a lopsided grin on his face.

Matt chuckled and raised his hand. "You can call me Matt, but I swear I'm not trying to take your job. Uncle Leo said I'd just shadow you. To learn. Before college. Right, Uncle Leo?

"Hey Matt. You probably shouldn't call Leo…" Brianna began scolding Matt.

"It's Leopold, and it's fine," Leopold interjected. He found he liked being called Uncle Leo. His lion liked it as well. Soon enough he and Brianna would be mated and married, so there was no reason not to be referred to as Uncle or *Zio* Leo now if Brianna's nieces and nephews wanted to call him that.

Josh raised a brow. Leopold shrugged. What could he do? That was family and the Palermos were his family now.

Josh extended his hand and Matt shook it eagerly. "If you say so, Matt. But I'll keep my eye on you." He extended his hand to Brianna. "It's a pleasure to meet you. Everyone is thrilled you're joining us today."

A pretty pink blush settled over Brianna's cheeks as she shook hands with Josh. "Oh. Well. That's very nice to hear. Thank you."

Josh handed them each sanctuary staff T-shirts. "I thought since you're shadowing me today, you should dress the part," he said, mostly for Matt's benefit.

Matt's eyes widened with an expression of disbelief. "Really? Cool!" He hurried and put the shirt on over the one he was already wearing, smoothing it down until he believed it looked perfect. Leopold and Brianna slipped theirs on and were ready for the day's activities.

Squealing meows from the apparently woken cubs filled the room.

"Oh, my gosh," Brianna said with a sense of wonder in her voice.

Josh led them to the pet pen. The tiger cub was squealing and stumbling around the enclosure, while the lion cub was still sucking on his pacifier, but following the tiger, its eyes partially opened.

"We just rescued them. They're a week old. Basher is the lion cub. Dasher is the tiger cub." Josh informed them.

"The tiger's eyes are closed. Why are their ears folded over like that?" Brianna asked Josh.

Josh turned to Matt who was watching the action inside the pen like a kid in a candy store. "Would you like to answer your aunt?" Was Josh testing the boy or giving him an opportunity to shine? Leopold hoped the latter.

Matt nodded. "Sure. *Zia*, they're babies. Their ears will pop up in a couple of weeks. Lion's eyes open a little sooner than tiger's. It'll take another week or two before Dasher's eyes open."

Basher ditched his pacifier and joined Dasher with screeching meows. The beginnings of what would eventually become roars for both of them. Leopold's lion wanted to join the cubs. He felt for his lion. It had been too long since he'd visited the sanctuary and allowed his lion to play.

"They're very vocal, huh?" Brianna's wide smile warmed Leopold's heart. She was enjoying herself. What a relief.

Josh chuckled. "It's feeding time."

"I call dibs on feeding Basher. Brianna can feed Dasher," Leopold proclaimed.

"Why doesn't that surprise me, My Lord?" Josh shook his head, a smirk curling his lips.

Brianna paled and her eyes grew wide. "What? No. I can't. I know they're cute, but they're…real."

Matt placed a comforting hand on Brianna's shoulder. "It'll be okay. Dasher's a baby. She can't hurt you. She doesn't even have teeth yet. Neither does Basher."

Brianna arched a brow. "Really?"

Josh nodded. "Matt knows his stuff. They're not able to retract their claws yet, so to avoid scratches or reduce possible scratching we'll give you a thick blanket. Let's wash up. The feeding chairs are to your left with blankets hanging on the backs. Matt, want to help me weigh them, get their milk ready and record everything in our computer system while they're being fed?"

"You bet I do!"

Leopold and Brianna observed the excited boy from their feeding chairs after they'd washed up. Matt hesitated a moment at the pen before deciding to begin with Dasher.

"Ladies first," Matt said. Poor, hungry Dasher squeaked up a storm when Matt picked her up, wiggling and thrashing as he carried her to the scale. "It's okay. *Zia's* going to feed you in a minute. Hold still just one second. Okay, Josh. Looks like three pounds, two ounces."

Matt placed Dasher back and brought a squirming Basher to the scale. "Basher is three pounds, six ounces."

"Yes. Mine's bigger." Leopold boasted.

Brianna rolled her eyes. "It's not a competition."

"Of course it is. Basher will be the king of the jungle one day," Leopold stated.

"But grown tigers are larger and weigh more

than grown lions do, Uncle Leo."

Brianna stuck her tongue out at him. Leopold shrugged. It was true after all.

Matt was an attentive student working with Josh to prepare the cub's milk formula and documenting how many ounces each cub would receive.

Josh brought a squirming and fussy Basher to Leopold with Matt following holding the formula bottle. With his blanket in place, he calmed the lion cub down once he got the bottle nipple in the cub's mouth. Matt pet Basher for a moment, before getting Dasher's bottle.

Brianna cautiously accepted a grunting and squealing Dasher. At least his mate was still smiling. It was a good sign. Dasher stopped fussing once she began drinking her formula, as Leopold expected.

A tear rolled down Brianna's cheek. Leopold and his lion panicked.

"Is Dasher hurting you?" Leopold was ready to call Josh over.

Brianna shook her head, her smile securely in place. "No. I just can't believe I'm feeding a baby tiger. Look at her little ears twitch. It's the most amazing thing ever. Thank you for trusting me with this."

He trusted his mate completely. "I wanted

you to see first-hand what the work you're doing means. In a literal sense. The visibility and donations the sanctuary and foundation are receiving. Where those donations will go. What the charity gala's outcome will mean."

Brianna nodded, snuggling Dasher a little closer. Her initial fears seemed to have disappeared and Leopold was grateful.

After the cubs had been fed, were back in their pen and dozing off, Leopold guided Brianna around the facility while Josh took Matt under his wing for more of a working experience.

Leopold led Brianna, while wearing a belt with a tranquilizer gun attached, through the interior corridors and animal enclosures which connected to the exterior habitats. Many of his employees had made a point of seeking them out and met his mate, with Brianna blushing all the while.

Matt and Josh met back up with them at the interior enclosure of Sasha the cheetah. His lion paced, excited to see his "sister." Leopold vowed to return soon so his lion could play with her.

"How was your time with Josh? Did you work hard? Have fun?" Brianna asked Matt. He sported a warm smile, so it couldn't have been too difficult for the enthusiastic boy.

"Yeah. It was so great. Well, except for the

cleaning the poop part inside the indoor cages. But I know everything needs to be clean for the animals, so it wasn't too bad." Matt nodded, seemingly not overly bothered by the poop cleaning part of his work. Good boy.

"I explained to Matt, no matter what job you have, there will always be parts of the job you like more than others. He did very well today. Whenever you're ready, your guests are on the other side of Sasha's outdoor habitat," Josh said and held his tranquilizer gun at the ready.

Brianna bit her lower lip, her eyes blinking rapidly.

"It'll be fine, mate. You'll be perfectly safe with us. I would never let anything happen to you or Matt. Sasha is sweet and gentle. You'll see," Leopold assured her.

She accepted Leopold's hand and he led them through the interior enclosure, the hay and straw crunching beneath their feet, to the exterior grassy habitat. He spotted Sasha playing with a large red ball near where his guests were watching. He heard her purr with is sensitive hearing.

As they drew closer, Sasha stopped playing and turned toward them. He felt Brianna's hand stiffen in his. He brushed his lips against hers and slowly approached the cheetah. His guests watched with widened eyes.

"Sweetheart. How are you? I know it's been a while." Leopold didn't have to wait long before the one-eyed cheetah began purring so loudly, he was certain everyone could hear.

She ran toward him, and Leopold caught her when she leaped at him. Everyone witnessing the scene gasped, except Josh.

Sasha's purrs intensified and she enthusiastically licked Leopold's face, obviously happy to see him. He chuckled and petted the joyful cheetah and she continued to shower him with affection. "It's all right. She's just happy to see me." He assured everyone. "I'm sorry I haven't visited until now. My lion will be back soon to play, all right?" He whispered to Sasha. She replied with more face licks.

Once she'd calmed down, Leopold directed Sasha's attention to Brianna. "See that beautiful girl? That's my mate. Do you understand? My *mate*." Leopold whispered.

Sasha's nose twitched, sniffing the air, still purring. Leopold waved Brianna over and held on to the scruff of Sasha's neck. With Josh by her side and his tranquilizer gun in hand, she slowly approached. Josh gestured for her to crouch down.

"She purrs so loud." Brianna whispered.

"She's a good girl, I told you." Leopold gently

guided the cheetah toward his mate, holding on tight to her scruff.

After a moment of hesitation, Sasha rubbed up against Brianna, purring happily. With a stunned expression, Brianna tentatively pet the wildcat, an expression of awe on her beautiful face.

They bid Sasha goodbye after a few minutes, needing to meet up with everyone for lunch. Leopold drove them, including Josh, to the sanctuary's Wildcat Café in their waiting golf cart after Brianna ensured Matt was securely buckled in the back seat.

They were greeted with cheers, back claps, and handshakes. Leopold assumed they'd all stopped by the gift shop and used their half-off discount. Many wore sanctuary logo T-shirts and ball caps. Many of the kids held lion, tiger, and other wildcat stuffed animals. It did his heart good to see all the smiling faces, young and older.

"Your VIP badges are good for complimentary lunch and beverages so eat and drink up!" Leopold announced. That earned him additional cheers.

Brianna's family pushed together enough tables so they could all sit together. Matt invited Josh to sit with them. Leopold couldn't have been prouder of Matt's kindness and graciousness. He was a special kid.

Over hearty sandwiches and other delicious treats the café had to offer, Matt excitedly detailed his day, including the not so fun poop cleaning part.

"And so, Josh said I could work at the sanctuary like a junior intern. And they'll pay me. Can I Mom and Dad? Please? I'll put half my money in my college fund." Matt bounced in his chair, hoping Lara and Tommy agreed.

Leopold would ensure the boy's college tuition would be fully paid for when the time came, but that was a conversation for another time and in private.

"But what about me?" Angel asked, nearly in tears.

Shit, he hadn't thought about the little girl. Of course she'd want to tag along with her big brother. Chloe had been the same way, even though she'd been older when she'd joined his family.

Josh piped up before Leopold could devise a solution. "I suggest we begin with two days a week, provided Matt and Angel keep their grades up at school. Angel, would you like to help out at the gift shop? You can help stock the cute stuffed animals, T-shirts, and other sanctuary mementos? You'll even get to wear a special gift shop shirt."

"Yay! Can I Mommy? Daddy?"

"If two days a week turns out to be too much, we can always scale back to one day." Josh offered, hoping to convince Lara and Tommy.

The doting parents shared a knowing glance and nodded. "Sure. I think it'll be good for the kids. Especially Matt," Lara said.

"I'll send a car for the kids, so you don't have to adjust your schedules. And I'll have healthy snacks ready for them." Leopold suggested. The last thing he wanted to do was upend their lives or inconvenience them.

"Thanks, man. We appreciate that." Tommy replied.

"Leepold, you doing a good thing here. Helping the animals. It was good idea to put the information about how you save them by their area." Brianna's father Aldo's eyes beamed with pride.

"Thank you, sir. With Brianna's help, we'll be able to do so much more." Leopold believed that wholeheartedly. She was already making a positive difference. Personally, as well as professionally.

"I'll be right back. I need more ketchup for my fries." Brianna excused herself.

Leopold retrieved a note from his pants pocket and placed it next to her partially eaten crispy chicken sandwich. It read: *Take me inside your wildest dreams, inside your wildest heart.* Her family didn't say a word but grinned at him.

His cell phone rang, interrupting his time with Brianna's family. His lion growled. *I agree, pal.* He recognized the El Salvadoran number on the phone's display and excused himself, moving toward the back of the café for privacy.

"Santos, how are you?" Leopold said, answering the call. Santos was the leader of the El Salvadoran faction of the North American Shifter Collective.

"I'm well. But more importantly, how are *you*? We've all heard you've met your mate but are you formally mated? The clock is ticking on the elders' deadline, my friend." Santos pointed out.

Leopold's gut clenched. He'd already heard from the faction leaders of Canada, Cuba, Belize, the Bahamas, Saint Lucia, and Panama. They'd all offered their support but had stopped short of pledging their loyalty if the elders stripped him of his leadership at the end of the year.

He caught a glance of Brianna as she sat down with her ketchup and read his love note. The smile on her face made his heart swell. He lived to see her smiles.

"Not formally mated yet, no. It's only a matter of time."

"Listen. I hate to put more pressure on you than you already have, but if the elders revoke your leadership, our faction can't stand by you. It's nothing personal, but we need the Syndicate's backing and support. I'm speaking not only for El Salvador but several other factions as well."

Anger swelled in Leopold's gut, and he snorted with derision. He squeezed his phone so tightly in his hand he was afraid he'd crush it. After everything he'd done for the organization, he'd expected more from the factions. "Fuck you. Of course it's personal."

"Perhaps the elders won't follow through on their threat if you're not formally mated, since for all intents and purposes, you and your mate are together."

Time would tell, but Leopold didn't give a shit. Their threats were bullshit, and he wouldn't disrespect his mate by pressuring her to mate with him before she was ready.

"Maybe, maybe not. But Santos, believe me when I tell you, I won't forget who stood by me and who betrayed me when the time comes."

Brianna toyed with Leopold's latest love note seated at her conference room table in her office, three weeks after their visit to the New York sanctuary. *If love is blind, I'll use my soul to see you and my heart to feel you.* The note had been tucked into a bouquet of orange tiger lilies delivered earlier in the day. Their subtle scent lingered in the air.

The New York club managers and Benjamin sat around the table with the new Chicago and Schaumburg club managers on a conference call with them.

Brianna reviewed her notes on her laptop. "It looks like we're on schedule for the grand openings in Illinois in two weeks. Renovations are just about finished, and we're fully staffed."

"Absolutely. Chicago is ready."

"Schaumburg residents are looking forward to the grand opening."

Brianna grinned. She got on well with the new Illinois club managers. They were personable, professional, and fully onboard with the company's long-term plans.

"A quick update on the loyalty programs. The cross promotions between the clubs, sanctuaries and Luxe hotels are making a huge difference in foundation donations and generating additional business for all three businesses." Brianna hadn't been sure at first but was thrilled with the results so far.

Everyone around the table nodded. Except for Kaylee who was fussing on her phone. Brianna had done her best to ignore and work around the black leopard shifter with the nasty attitude, but it had become more and more difficult to do lately.

As Brianna and Leopold spent more time together, Kaylee became ruder and shorter with her. Brianna spent most nights with Leopold, either at his place or her condo, finding it nearly impossible to sleep well without him beside her. That pesky mating bond hard at work on her.

Although Brianna was certain she was in love with him, mating bond or not, she couldn't help but believe Leopold would be better off mating with someone else. Someone who could help him fulfill his shifter obligations and satisfy the Syndicate elders. Someone other than Kaylee. The thought of him mating with someone else made her sick to her stomach, but she still believed it was the best option. The wise option. Leopold disagreed.

He'd vowed to stay by her side regardless of what the elders did at the end of the year. She hoped he wasn't making a mistake. He had so much to lose, regardless of his claims not to care as long as he had her in his life. At times, the guilt she felt about it all was overwhelming.

"The updated online scheduling system has gone over really well too. It's a lot more organized and the staff likes it a lot better than the old system. They can work together to cover each other and its less managerial overhead." Benjamin's support was always welcomed.

Kaylee rolled her eyes and tossed her phone on the table. Shit. Brianna braced herself for Kaylee's inevitable tirade. She was so tired of her crap.

"Will you all stop kissing up to her? Everything was fine before Brianna got here, you know." Kaylee lashed out.

To Brianna's relief, everyone around the table shook their heads.

"That's not true, things are much better since she got here."

"Business is better."

"The employees are happier."

"Oh, get off it!" Kaylee glared at Brianna with fury in her eyes. "You think you're so high and mighty? You're nothing special. I have a drawer full of Leopold's little love notes."

Brianna realized Kaylee was angry and lashing out, but her outburst still hurt. Whatever happened between Kaylee and Leopold before

Brianna got involved with him didn't really matter. She may have been unsure about their future, but she was sure Leopold loved her. Thanks to their mating bond, she felt his love. It was strong and unwavering.

She was also sure she'd had it with Kaylee. The woman wasn't fit to work for The Lion's Den in any capacity, especially a managerial one. "I'd rather have done this in private, but you've left me no choice. You're fired. Go back to your club and pack your things. You're finished at The Lion's Den."

Brianna felt a sense of satisfaction when Kaylee's eyes nearly bugged out of her skull. *Serves you right, bitch.*

"You can't fire me." Kaylee snarled.

"I have complete autonomy to hire and fire as I see fit. You know that." Brianna reminded her.

Kaylee turned to Benjamin, presumably planning on pleading her case to him.

Good luck. He doesn't like you either.

"You're the beta. Do something." Kaylee begged.

Benjamin merely shrugged, keeping his expression neutral. "I'm not going to do a fucking thing. It's beyond my paygrade, anyway. Brianna should have fired you weeks ago. I can't believe she's tolerated your shitty attitude and obnoxious behavior as long as she has."

"I agree," Leopold said from her office doorway. "Find a job that's not at a pride affiliated company. You'll be provided a letter of recommendation, but don't push your luck."

Kaylee bolted out of her chair; her face marred in anger and paced Brianna's office with her hands clenched into fists. "You're acting like a fool over someone who doesn't even want you. You have so much to lose and over what? A *human*? You'll end up regretting it."

Brianna held back a giggle. Leopold appeared bored with Kaylee's tantrum.

"I doubt that. You heard Brianna. Go back to your club and pack your things. You're through." Leopold entered Brianna's office, leaving the doorway clear for Kaylee and crossed his arms.

Kaylee pursed her lips and grabbed her phone off the conference table. She tossed Brianna one last murderous glance and left without another word. Although she was relieved, she wouldn't have to interact with Kaylee any longer, Brianna suspected they hadn't seen or heard the last of her.

Thirty minutes later, after her meeting had concluded and everyone had left, Leopold closed and locked her office door. His gaze, dark with longing was laser focused on her. His masculine energy dominated her as it always did.

She leaned against her desk, as a lusty feeling of warmth stole over her. His eyes caressed her while he approached with a stealthy, feline grace she'd come to understand.

"You were so sexy when you wielded your power over Kaylee earlier." Leopold lifted her onto her desk. His lips met hers in a slow, drugging kiss.

"Really?" she breathed after their kiss ended, wet heat flaring between her legs.

"Hell, yes." His mouth recaptured hers, showering kisses on her lips and along her jaw. He lifted the soft, flowing skirt of her summer dress up her thighs while he continued kissing her with reckless abandon.

She shivered in delight when he slipped a deft finger inside her lace panties and ran it along her drenched pussy. He growled, making her pulse race.

Brianna held him tightly as he stroked her sensitive clit, her entire body on fire with pleasure. So close to release, Leopold rubbed her clit in torturous circles until she came in cascading waves. Her orgasm hitting her full force. She cried out, unconcerned if anyone heard her. It was her office, and she was with the alpha. No one had better say a word.

Leopold licked his finger clean and moaned. When he unbuckled his belt, unzipped, and pulled his hard cock out of his pants, Brianna opened her legs wider, eager to feel his thick length inside of her.

He pushed forward filling her completely with one forceful thrust. Leopold was impossibly big, hurting her in the best of ways. Brianna wrapped her legs around his thighs, and they moved together as one. His cock plunged in and out of her, searing her like a brand, making her breasts bounce.

Brianna's inner muscles gripped him tighter, melting around him. Her mighty alpha grunted and groaned as he fucked her. Leopold drove in and out of her with an animal fierceness she'd come to crave. Her pussy clenched and rippled around him, her every nerve ending quivering. The tension inside her exploded and she gave into the moment in complete surrender. She called out his name in ecstasy as he leaned his head back and roared, filling her with his warm cum.

He gathered her against him, as their breathing slowly returned to normal. She felt deliciously sore basking in the blissful afterglow.

"You are like water, keeping me alive, keeping me afloat, and thirsting for you. I love you, mate," Leopold whispered and brushed his lips against her damp forehead.

Kaylee's spiteful parting words echoed in Brianna's brain. She hoped love would be enough and Leopold wouldn't come to regret sticking with her.

Chapter Eleven

Leopold washed his hands in the powder room near his front door. He checked his suit jacket in the mirror. Not a speck of lint. His thick golden locks, lay perfectly as they usually did. His lion tilted his head upward, showing off his mane. It was good to be the alpha.

It was mid-October and true to his word, his Uncle Hendrick was retiring after a long and distinguished career in the army. He and Brianna were due to leave shortly for the Claverack compound, where his grandparents were throwing Hendrick's retirement party.

A smile curved his lips at thoughts of his precious mate. Brianna spent most nights with him and Prissy now. She'd helped him redecorate some and had transformed his house into a home. Leopold thanked fate for her every day. It pained him to know she still had doubts about their future and spent an occasional night alone at her condo, considering he had no doubts whatsoever. He was certain she'd consent to be his mate eventually. The love he felt from her was intense and true. It was only a matter of time.

The consent timing didn't matter much to him now. Leopold was rather curious if the elders would follow through on their threats at the end of December. In some ways, he welcomed the freedom to only pursue *his* interests, and not everyone else's.

Leopold startled when the doorbell rang. He wasn't expecting anyone. He exited the bathroom and noticed a small gold box with a red ribbon wrapped around it on one of the foyer tables. That was odd, it hadn't been there when he'd stepped into the powder room.

Benjamin stood on the other side of his door; his eyebrows drawn together in an anguished expression. "You heard already?" Benjamin asked.

What? He gestured toward the mystery package. "This showed up while I was in the bathroom."

They both stared at the box, as if it were a bomb. Slowly they moved toward it and sniffed the air. Brianna? Benjamin grabbed the box and held it up to his nose.

"Looks like a present from your mate." Without asking, Benjamin began opening it.

Leopold snatched it from his beta. Brianna had given him a gift? No woman had ever given him a gift before, other than family. He wasn't sure how to feel. "That's mine. Back off." He tore at the gold wrapping and opened the white box underneath. He retrieved a white coffee cup filled with Hershey Kisses and with a cartoon outline of a cat on it that read *Life is Better With a Cat*. A laugh broke free from his chest. He loved his gift. He wouldn't drink his coffee or tea out of anything else from now on.

"Sweet." Benjamin helped himself, without asking, to a chocolate treat and popped it in his mouth.

Leopold moved his treat-filled cup away from his beta. "This is mine. And what did you mean when you said I heard already?"

Benjamin ran a hand through his hair as his forehead creased with concern. "We've lost track of Kaylee."

Leopold's men had been keeping tabs on her since she'd been fired from The Lion's Den. She'd secured a manager's position thanks to his connections and recommendation at Guillaume's, an authentic French bistro. He'd been told Kaylee had been well behaved, low key since her firing. He didn't trust her for a second though. *A woman scorned, right?*

"You think she'd be stupid enough to try something *today* of all days? At the compound?" She'd never survive if she did.

Benjamin shrugged and shook his head. "Oliver didn't want to take any chances. A few of us are following your car to the compound, and we've increased compound patrol, as a precaution. Everyone's on alert. We'll find out what she's up to."

"Get out of here before Brianna comes down. I don't want to upset her with this."

Benjamin stole three more chocolates before he slipped out the door.

Brianna's tempting scent tickled his nose before he saw her at the top of the stairs. His mate's deep purple, curve hugging, off the shoulder, geometric patterned sweater dress nearly made him drool. Her soft, dark curls flowed loosely around her shoulders.

God, she's beautiful.

Her eyes sparkled when she noticed he was holding her gift. Leopold kissed her cheek when she reached him.

"I love my gift, and I love you," Leopold assured her.

A pretty blush tinted her cheeks. "I know it's a silly thing, but when I saw it, I just had to get it. I have one too. So we match. What's wrong?"

Damn. The mating bond was a blessing but also a curse at times. "Nothing's wrong. Just anxious to get on the road so we have some time to relax before the party." It wasn't a lie. Just not the entire truth.

Leopold got his mate, his sleeping kitten tucked inside her carrier with her favorite toys, and their bags safely into their waiting Mercedes-Maybach limousine. He was grateful Brianna hadn't noticed their protection detail nearby.

After they'd been on the road a few minutes and settled in, he presented Brianna with one of his special notes. It read: *You can excite me by doing nothing at all, just by being you*. And it was true.

A small grin stole across her full, glossy lips. "Do you have a handle on the guest list today?"

She'd expressed her concern about who'd be attending the party several times already. "The Mayor of Albany, the Governor of New York, the Secretary of State, a slew of military big wigs, family, friends, family in from overseas including my grandparents, a few of the alphas from around the country and from countries in the

North American Shifter Collective. Hendrick's biggest fan, your brother Vito." A sigh escaped his lips. "And some members of the International Shifter Syndicate that include family." He suspected she wouldn't be pleased. Truth be told, he wasn't looking forward to seeing anyone from the ISS either.

Brianna lowered her head, her face sagging. "I hope no one makes issue with our mating *situation*. This party isn't about us."

"I assure you it's going to be fine. Haven't my grandparents been friendly and welcoming during our video calls?" They'd been cordial and warm toward his mate during their many video calls.

"They have. Maybe everyone's waiting to see me in person. To get me alone and give me a piece of their mind about us."

Leopold clasped her warm hand in his and kissed her knuckles. "I don't believe that will happen. The focus will be on Hendrick. He'll make sure of it." He was more concerned about Kaylee but couldn't voice his worries out loud. "Let's just relax, enjoy the party, eat some good food and unwind over the weekend. You deserve a break and my lion's looking forward to roaming and playing on the property with Prissy."

Brianna nodded; a nervous smile played

along the edges of her lips.

After a thankfully uneventful ride to Claverack, he and Brianna had unpacked in his cottage, freshened up and joined the party with Prissy in her carrier in tow. He'd left the door open for her so she could retreat inside when she needed some space away from all the guests and festivities. Leopold wished he had that option. Hours of doting on Hendrick wasn't his idea of a good time. The sooner the party was over and he had his mate all to himself again in his cottage, the better.

Leopold held Brianna's hand as they made the rounds and mingled. They both stood and watched an interesting scene play out across the room. Chloe was blushing, Vito looked confused, but couldn't keep his eyes off Chloe, and Mason appeared annoyed at them.

"Vito and Chloe?" Brianna whispered excitely.

"It's possible." If his sister and Brianna's brother turned out to be fated mates, Leopold saw no problem with it. They'd be lucky to have each other. Mason would have to understand and bow out.

Everyone sat for dinner and focused on his grandfather as he stood with a champagne glass in his hand.

"Thank you all for joining us today. When my boy informed his mother and I of his plans to join the military after college, I'll be honest, we were stunned. But as the years went on it became clear that serving this wonderful country our family has called home for centuries now, Hendrick had made the right decision. He's served this country honorably and has made our family incredibly proud. And although this chapter of your life is coming to an end son, may the next be as rewarding and fulfilling as the previous. Best of luck, my boy."

Party guests applauded and toasted his uncle. Government and military officials added words of praise to Hendrick's service. His own personal feelings aside, Leopold wished him well in his future endeavors. There was serious consideration being made for Hendrick becoming Defense Secretary somewhere down the line. He'd already booked multiple speaking engagements and was nearly finished writing his memoirs. His uncle would be just fine.

Leopold enjoyed a delicious meal with Brianna and his parents seated around him. It was a comforting glimpse into what the future held, regardless of leadership threats.

"I'd say things are going exceptionally well with the club as of late. From the successful Illinois grand openings, the upcoming openings in Los Angeles, San Diego, and San Francisco and the extraordinary outcome of the charity gala last month, I'd say the future is looking bright." Leopold's father raised his champagne glass and toasted his mate.

Leopold couldn't have agreed more. The charity gala had gone exceptionally well, raised awareness for the sanctuaries and had generated substantial donations for his foundation. Thanks to Dirk's efforts, the press coverage had been insane, generating invitation inquiries from celebrities around the globe.

Brianna's lips curved with a gracious smile. "Thank you, Willem. I agree. Phoenix and Tucson will follow the California openings and we're considering a location in Las Vegas."

"Have you considered expanding to other countries like Canada, the Bahamas, Belize, St. Lucia? The possibilities are endless, don't you agree?" his mother asked, her eyes beaming with excitement.

Had his mother intentionally mentioned countries within the Collective that were supporting him in the midst of the elders' chaos? Brianna seemed to consider his mother's suggestion for a moment.

Brianna gazed at him thoughtfully. "I know

we haven't spoken about LVH Luxe Hotel expansion plans, but what do you think about making the clubs part of new Luxe Hotel properties in those countries?"

His mother gasped. "I love that idea. What do you think, son?"

Leopold thought, no, he *knew* he was the luckiest man in the world. His mate was amazing. He reached over and clasped Brianna's hand, giving it a gentle squeeze.

"I think my woman is brilliant." Brianna's triumphant smile was Leopold's reward.

Brianna sipped on a frothy cappuccino, off to the side, away from the bulk of the party guests. She needed a moment to reflect on the events of the day.

According to Chloe, Vito was her fated mate. How he'd react to *that* revelation, Brianna had no idea. Brianna adored Chloe and would welcome her into the Palermo family happily, once the dust settled with her big brother.

Brianna had braced herself for at least one confrontation from a family member in the International Shifter Syndicate. When several members had approached her together, to her surprise and amusement, they'd wanted to know how to get on next year's charity gala guest list. She diplomatically explained she'd used an internet list randomizing program to be fair and unbiased with family member selections. They had been disappointed but had commended her sense of fairness.

She should have been relieved no one had mentioned her and Leopold's prospective mating, but she was bothered for some reason. He'd been patient and considerate with her about how she wanted to move their relationship forward because he was certain she would.

Brianna was afraid Leopold would lose his leadership positions if she waited much longer. What kind of person would she be if she allowed him to lose everything he'd worked so hard for? He winked at her from across the room and her stomach fluttered.

Feeling overwhelmed by her emotional struggle, she snuck out of the room and headed to the parlor room where she'd left her flats and a jacket. Prissy's carrier was on the floor near her shoes. The kitten had retreated to her safe place about an hour before. Brianna took a quick peek inside to find the precious black kitten asleep among her toys.

She spotted something inside one of her flats

as she approached them. A small message in a bottle? With sand and tiny shells? Her lips curved into a grin. Leopold had stepped up his game. She removed the bottle's cork and retrieved the message.

More Than Just A Cat

I'm hoping that this poem is the thing
to show a lion's more than just a cat
left pacing in his cage. A diplomat
in love's the surest conqueror, the king,
the one who knows to roar is not to sing—
and so, here is my song. One caveat:
my whole heart's here, but you could leave it flat.
My whole heart's here and you could make it sting.
My heart is something easy to destroy.
My heart is something easy to deceive.
It's brave and true. It's like an asteroid
that flares so bright it never stops to grieve,
but burns to ashes in its quest for joy:
all yours to love, if only you believe.

Brianna slipped her flats on, grabbed her jacket, and hurried outside. A wave of light-headedness came over her and her ears rung. It was all too much. She followed the cobblestone path from the main house and private cottages through the wooded acreage on the property and to the pond. It was just too much, she thought as her insides quivered and her chest tightened. Leopold was too much.

She collapsed on the padded seat facing the pond. The calm and serenity were exactly what she'd needed. A few solitary minutes to get her head on straight before it got dark and she had to return to the party.

Brianna thought she'd heard a twig snap nearby and rolled her eyes. She'd noticed Benjamin and others follow them on the drive to the compound but hadn't said anything. Leopold was protective of her and suspected pride members were watching over her now. She was grateful they hadn't invaded her space and remained out of sight.

What was wrong with her? Why was she finding it so difficult to commit to Leopold? She was certain she didn't ever want to be with anyone else, the mating bond was strong between them. Maybe she was looking for a guarantee after her marriage to Grayson had failed so spectacularly. But she knew there were no guarantees. The mating bond might be the closest thing to a guarantee she could hope for.

She felt her cell phone in the jacket pocket. She dialed Jilly, hoping she had a minute to talk.

"Hey, how's the party? Is Vito fanboying bad?" Jilly's chuckle brought a smile to Brianna's face.

"He hasn't been too bad. It's been good. The guest list is surreal, but everyone's been very nice." That much was true. Brianna had felt like she'd belonged among Leopold's family, friends, and high-profile guests.

"Then what's wrong? Did something happen with you and Leo? Something's been bothering you lately."

"I'm scared, I guess. Of taking things to the next level. My marriage to Grayson was a wreck. I couldn't go through that again. All of your marriages are perfect, and Leo and I are so different, you know?" Jilly didn't, not in the ways Brianna meant. She hadn't told anyone in her family that Leopold's family were shifters or that they'd all been living amongst shifters and hadn't even known it.

Jilly's laugh surprised her. "Perfect? *No one's* marriage is perfect, even the good ones. Because no one is perfect. There's always give and take. Compromises. What matters is that you're with someone who will have your back, even when you don't agree."

Brianna supposed that was true. She hadn't

experienced it in her marriage to Grayson though. Rather the opposite.

"I know his family is different because they're uber-wealthy. I couldn't even imagine what that must be like. But they're a lot like us too, in the ways that matter. They work hard, they're loyal and they value family. And Bree, love doesn't need to be perfect. It just needs to be true. Real. And most importantly, Leo isn't Grayson. Not even close."

Jilly was right on all counts. Brianna was getting in her own way. She'd stopped comparing the two men weeks ago, because there was no comparison. She ended her call with Jilly feeling lighter than she had since learning about shifters, Leopold, and what they were to each other.

"With that smile on your face, you must be thinking about me."

The hair on the back of Brianna's neck stood on end and her stomach clenched. She bolted off the bench and whirled around.

"Grayson?" Brianna was stunned. How had he gotten on the compound? The sun was beginning to set, but she could clearly see his blond hair had thinned and he'd put on weight since she'd left him. Although petty, she felt a sense of satisfaction that he'd suffered. He'd caused her enough pain to last two lifetimes.

He rounded the bench to face her, and she stepped back. Where *was* everyone?

"How did you find me?" *Leo where are you?* Could he sense her distress from inside the main house?

His sinister smirk made her skin crawl. "Your good friend Kaylee Hart."

Brianna's stomach churned. She should have known. Kaylee had had it out for her from the beginning.

"It's time for you to come back home to California where you belong. You've played long enough. You and I both know you don't belong here, with the Van Housens, no less. I did you a favor by marrying you. I didn't realize you'd set your sights higher and had become such a gold-digging tramp."

On instinct, she slapped Grayson. Hard. And her hand stung like hell afterwards.

Grayson stunned her and slapped Brianna so hard she fell back, landing on the hard ground. She touched her stinging cheek, tears pooling in her eyes.

"You fucking bitch. Who do you think you are?" Grayson barked out.

The growling and hissing caused them to turn their heads in its direction. Kaylee as her black leopard circled them, baring her fangs.

Brianna hurried to her feet, dread washing over her.

"Leo!" Brianna prayed someone heard her. She'd learned shifters had sensitive hearing.

A cowardly Grayson moved behind Brianna, using her as a shield. "What the fuck is going on?"

Was he serious? "You idiot. That's Kaylee."

"What are you talking about? Kaylee is a gorgeous brunette and a wildcat in bed."

Brianna felt nauseous. What had she ever seen in him? He was repugnant.

Kaylee stalked over to them, her growls louder. Grayson grabbed Brianna by the hips, and she shoved him away.

Brianna kept her expression neutral but was beyond relieved when Chloe, as her snow leopard, raced toward Kaylee, followed by other animals in Leopold's pride – various big cats, wolves, and others.

She moved out of the way as Chloe leaped onto Kaylee's back and clamped down on her neck with her canines. They both hissed and growled as they rolled around on the ground, attacking each other.

Leopold, her beautiful lion alpha quickly ate up the distance between himself and the other pride animals racing toward her with Prissy running beside him. It was a sight to behold.

"Leopold stop!" Hendrick shouted, chasing him as a human with Vito following behind him, a bewildered expression on his face. This wasn't how she'd imagined Vito would learn about shifters.

A wolf she presumed was Mason, a leopard, and a white tiger she presumed was Daniel, rushed Chloe, knocked her off Kaylee, immobilizing the angry black leopard. Bright red spots dotted Chloe's white fur.

Leopold reached them, jumped on Grayson, both of them tumbling to the ground. Leopold's thunderous roar made Grayson cry out in fear. Prissy growled and hissed at her ex.

"Brianna! Help me!" Grayson shrieked.

"Oh, but what can a gold-digging tramp like me do to help you?" Brianna couldn't help herself, she hated him so. She picked up the stressed kitten and tried to comfort her as she cried and licked her face.

Hendrick shifted into his lion, bursting out of his clothes. Vito stopped dead in his tracks, his jaw falling open. Poor guy.

Hendrick shoved against Leopold until he slid off Grayson. Leopold attacked Hendrick, drawing blood on his uncle's chest and legs. They snarled and grunted as they fought each other. Leopold was the obvious stronger and more skilled fighter.

"General, you have to stop." Vito called out beside her. "What the fuck is going on?"

"Vito, please help me." Grayson begged, still sprawled on the ground, crying and bleeding from small cuts on his neck.

Vito glanced down at Grayson in disgust. "Go fuck yourself, asshole." Vito glared at her expectedly.

"Um...animal shifters exist? Leo is the alpha of the Van Housen pride, and I'm his fated mate." There was more, but Brianna wasn't sure her brother could handle it at the moment.

Leopold shifted back to his human form with Hendrick following. Leopold shoved Hendrick, but he didn't shove back.

"What the fuck are you doing? Are you challenging me for leadership? *Again*? Do you really think you could have done better than I've done for the pride and our family business if *you'd* taken over ten years ago?"

Brianna's mouth fell open. *Hendrick* had challenged him ten years ago?

Hendrick bowed his head. "No, Your Majesty."

Leopold growled in Hendrick's face. "You're

damned right. I showed you mercy once. I won't do it again. Your parents and brother won't convince me otherwise."

Head still bowed; Hendrick spoke again. "It was a blow to my ego when Willem chose you to take his place. I can admit that. But you've been a wonderful leader. I'm thinking about you and your mate. Killing her ex-husband could damage your relationship."

Leopold snorted and picked Grayson up off the ground by the throat. Grayson shook in Leopold's grasp. "If I had wanted this fucker dead, he'd be dead." Leopold narrowed his eyes, setting a dark, lethal stare on Grayson. "If you *ever* come near Brianna, her family or mine, or mention anything about what you've seen here today, I'll end you. Understand?"

Tears ran down Grayson's cheeks. "Yes, sir." Grayson whimpered.

Leopold let go of Grayson and turned to Benjamin who was back in human form. "Get him out of here."

Benjamin nodded, grabbed Grayson by the arm and led him away. Good riddance, Brianna thought.

"Everyone shift back," Leopold ordered his pride.

Brianna thought Vito was going to faint as all

the animals surrounding them shifted back into their nude human bodies, including Chloe. He rushed to her, offering her his jacket to cover her naked, blood-streaked form.

Leopold approached Kaylee, held by Daniel and Mason. If looks could kill, she would have been dead on the spot.

Genuine or not, tears streamed down Kaylee's face. Brianna didn't care and felt no sympathy for the bitch.

"She doesn't even want you. I would have been the perfect mate for you. She's been so disrespectful. She and her entire family call you Leo for fuck's sake." Kaylee rambled.

"It's an endearment! I've given you multiple opportunities since fate brought my mate to me out of respect for your parents." Leopold shook his head. "I call for the excommunication of Kaylee Hart from the Van Housen pride and the North American Shifter Collective."

"No, please don't do that." Kaylee sobbed; Brianna believed in earnest this time.

"I answer the call," Hendrick responded.

"I answer the call," Mason responded.

"I answer the call," Daniel responded.

Every shifter present also answered the call.

"Let it be acknowledged, the call for excommunication has been affirmed. Daniel. Mason.

Get Kaylee out of my sight and on a plane immediately."

Kaylee was dragged away, pleading for reconsideration.

Moments later, a naked Leopold wrapped his arms around Brianna. Prissy purred happily between them. "Are you all right, mate?"

Brianna brushed her lips against his. "I just needed a minute alone to think. I love you, Leopold."

"It's Leo." A cocky grin spread across Leopold's handsome face.

Brianna giggled. "I've been yours since the day we met, I just couldn't admit it. You are the water to my ocean. The twinkle in my eye. The blue in my sky. The sweet in my dreams. The beat of my heart. The love of my life. There's no reason to lose your leadership because of me. If you're willing to take a chance on me, I consent to being your mate."

"The only thing that matters to me is *you* and you're not a risk, you're a sure thing." Leopold captured Brianna's lips in a punishingly intense and beautiful kiss. "To our queen!"

Roars, hollers, and howls filled the air.

"And now, on to the mating." Leopold waggled his brows. A shiver of excitement rippled through her.

Chapter Twelve

With cheers and catcalls following behind them, Leopold led Brianna by the hand, proudly naked, back to his private cottage after she'd handed Prissy over to Chloe. A crazy, out-of-control fire burned hot inside of her.

When they reached his cottage and Leopold closed the door behind them, a wave of apprehension washed over Brianna. Although Chloe had explained the *simple* mechanics around mating and the mating mark, she struggled to fight her fear. She knew receiving the mark would hurt, even if only briefly.

Leopold faced her, with a sinful grin on his lips. "Don't be afraid, my mate." Their mouths came together in a scorching kiss. He tasted like power, and risk, and wicked savage desire longing to break free. Her core slickened in anticipation of what came next.

Brianna's body pulsed with heat as they inched their way, hand in hand to the master bedroom. Leopold placed a soft kiss on her forehead. "Someone's overdressed. Take all this off and get into bed. I'll be right back." Leopold winked and disappeared into the en suite master bath.

She removed her jacket and stripped out of her sweater dress and purple lacey lingerie while she heard the water running in the bathroom. Brianna slipped into the bed; the silk sheets cool against her overheated skin. Excitement warred with trepidation as she waited for Leopold.

Her heart turned over in her chest when the water shut off. This was it, in a few minutes her life would irrevocably change forever. Was she ready for that? Her first inclination was to run, but her soul kept her right where she was. Where she truly believed she belonged.

Leopold emerged from the bathroom bare chested, dressed in a red, white, blue, and orange tartan kilt with a furry, tasseled sporran pouch hanging from a chain around his hips. She couldn't quite decipher the embellished silver arced cantle along the top of the sporran from her spot on the bed.

God he was gorgeous, and all hers. She wasn't sure what she'd done to deserve him, but she was through questioning it.

A flicker of a smile passed her lips as a burst of giggles escaped. "What's all this? A kilt?" She didn't understand.

Leopold stalked over to the bed as if she were his prey. She supposed in a way she indeed was. In a sexy sort of way.

He gazed at Brianna with eyes full of trust, love, and pride. "For you. I am your Viking steed."

Her mouth fell open. But...

"I heard you and the girls talking the first time I joined you for Sunday dinner. Sensitive shifter hearing, remember?"

She felt the heat of a blush on her neck and cheeks. Brianna remembered that conversation with her sisters-in-law very well in fact.

"You didn't have to do this for me. I didn't think the Dutch or the Netherlands had a tartan or wore kilts." Brianna was blown away by the thoughtful gesture.

Leopold crawled onto the bed, his gaze turning feral and possessive. Heat consumed her, pulsing through her veins.

"Ah, but we do. Our tartan combines the colors of the Netherlands red, white, and blue flag with orange, honoring the founder of the Netherlands. It's officially registered under the International Tartan Index of the Scottish Tartans Authority."

Leopold sealed his lips over Brianna's in a deep, all-consuming kiss. Sparks danced in the space between them, making her shiver in delight.

"It was designed for us to wear at Scottish events like the annual Dutch Whisky Festival. The silver cantle arc incorporates the dual lion Netherlands rampant or coat of arms. But in *my* case, the tartan is specifically used to claim my mate."

"Oh," slipped from Brianna's lips.

Leopold brushed a gentle kiss across her lips before reclaiming them in a more demanding, urgent kiss. He lowered her fully onto the bed and positioned himself on top of her. He was hot, heavy, and comforting at the same time. And all hers.

"And in case there was any doubt, I'm a *real* man wearing a kilt."

Goosebumps raced up Brianna's arms. He pressed his lips to hers, devouring her eager mouth. Leopold's kisses were soft and tender, then rough and greedy. Anticipation buzzed like a live wire between them.

Brianna slipped her hands under Leopold's kilt, seeking out the proof of his manliness. Her hands glided over his thighs until they reached the tight, toned bare globes of his ass, his muscles flexing beneath her fingers. She squeezed them, and a low guttural sound rumbled through his chest.

His warm lips began to explore her soft flesh. The touch of his lips around her pebbled nipple was a delicious sensation. Lust thrummed through her when he tugged gently and worked the other with his fingers.

Leopold nipped, licked, and nibbled his way down to Brianna's center. She eagerly spread her thighs to accommodate his wide shoulders.

His tongue quickly found her engorged clit and fired off short little licks and sucks. Brianna ran her hands through his lush hair, soft moans and mewls leaving her lungs. Leopold teased and worked her over until she gasped in sweet agony when her climax overtook her.

He glanced up at her with a cocky glint in his eyes, and a know-it-all grin on his lips. Her legs trembled when Leopold moved himself against her, teasing her damp folds open with his hard cock.

Leopold's jaw was clenched, but he offered Brianna a reassuring nod. Butterflies took flight deep in her belly. Her pussy fluttered around his thick length when he thrust deep inside of her. They moved together as one, her pussy stretched wider than she thought possible.

His strokes were sure, slow, and possessive with each hard thrust sending her reeling. Leopold groaned and pulled out nearly all the way, then drove back in. His cock was ruthless, plowing in and out of her, driving deep. He fucked her with such determination the delicious friction penetrated her every nerve.

Brianna and Leopold were pure heat and passion, fueling each other's desire. As her release tore through her, and Leopold surrendered to his own, she felt the burning sting of his mating bite where her neck and shoulder met.

She cried out, squeezing her eyes closed. Brianna wept, feeling Leopold's and his lion's love and joy as they became one, permanently solidifying their bond. In that moment, she emotionally experienced their happy future before her. Working together, playing together, a family – everything she'd ever wanted but was certain she'd never have after her disastrous years in California. He licked and kissed the spot where he'd marked her, easing the pain away.

She was surprised to gaze into Leopold's tear dampened eyes when she opened hers. Alarm bells rang in her head.

"What's the matter? Did we do it wrong?" Were they not mated? Had he been mistaken, and they weren't fated mates after all? She'd been convinced they were destined to be together. Despair twisted and turned inside of her.

Leopold's lips curved into a contented smile. "We did it exactly right, mate. Did you feel my emotions? My lion's? Did you sense our future together? The mated males tried to explain it to me, but I didn't really believe them."

Hope bloomed inside her. Everything would be fine. Better than fine. It would be amazing. "Yes. To everything."

Leopold gave her lower lip a hungry little nibble. "Good. We're joined forever now. You're my queen. The pride's queen. I'll stand behind you because I trust you to lead the way. I'll lead the way because I know you'll always have my back."

Fresh tears stung her eyes. "I love you so much."

Leopold showered her lips with feather light kisses. "I love you too, sweet mate."

Brianna felt bereft when he pulled out, left the

bed, and rifled through his weekend bag. She bolted upright when he returned to the bed with a small black velvet box in his hand. Her heart turned over. He was going to propose? A rush of emotions bubbled up inside her.

Leopold sat down beside her. "From a shifter's perspective, we're mated. But from a human's perspective." He opened the box and revealed the most beautiful, and enormous platinum set, emerald cut engagement ring with trillion cut stones on either side. "I'd like for you to be my wife." He removed the ring from the box and held it toward her, his hand shaking slightly.

"It's never been about the money for me, you know that. You didn't need to get me such a large ring." She loved it, but she loved Leopold and their life together more.

He raised a brow and put it back in the box. "That's too bad since I have a matching pendant and earrings for you to wear on our wedding day. A wedding day that will be worthy of the queen you are." A small smile twitched on his lips.

Brianna reached toward the box, giggling. "Let's not be hasty. I didn't say I didn't *want* it." She held her left hand out.

He slipped it on her ring finger and Brianna's heart beat wildly inside her ribs. Their wedding day couldn't come soon enough. A quick kiss sealed the deal. They were mated *and* engaged.

She and Leopold turned their heads when they heard scratching at the bedroom door. She suspected it was Prissy, missing them, needing cuddles.

Next came a knock at the door. What the heck? "Can't the alpha and his queen have a moment of peace?" He grabbed a white T-shirt from his bag and Brianna quickly slipped it on. He sat on the edge of the bed and sighed. "Enter."

Chloe held Prissy and cautiously stepped inside. Their black cat struggled against Chloe until she put her down on the bed. She purred and snuggled as they both pet her.

"Sorry to interrupt, but I wanted to let you know Uncle Hendrick's decided we should expand his retirement party to include your engagement. Vito's calling your family to see who's free to join us here at the compound."

Brianna shook her head. Although she appreciated Hendrick's kind gesture, it wouldn't work. "It'll be hours before they can get here."

Chloe and Leopold exchanged an amused, knowing glance. "It won't take long at all. Our transportation fleet includes helicopters." Leopold informed her.

Brianna rolled her eyes. "Of course it does."

Brianna tossed a few Hershey Kisses into Leo the lion's open mouth and popped one into her own. They enjoyed their sweet treats relaxing in the sunroom on an unusually warm mid-October afternoon, a year to the day after they'd gotten engaged.

A lot had happened over the course of twelve months. There were times she didn't recognize or believe her life. Prissy purred in delight, snuggled up against her protruded belly, while Brianna performed kitty massage on the cat's head and ears. She'd found a cat spa video online and discovered Prissy loved the spa treatments.

A lion's paw found its way onto her belly. Brianna stroked the soft fur. The lion was just as protective as the man of the twins that were due next week.

Brianna had been convinced it would take months to conceive after she'd stopped taking her birth control pills. Leopold believed otherwise. He was the alpha and alphas made babies – quickly.

And as if his ego needed more stoking, he'd knocked her up almost immediately after the doctor had given them the green light to try. Leopold had also been certain they'd conceived a boy because well – alphas made boys. When they'd learned she was carrying the alpha's twins, there was no way to bring him back down to earth. Twin boys, he was certain of it. He'd called everyone with the happy news.

He'd seen no point in using an ultrasound to confirm the future twin alpha's genders since he'd been convinced, they were male. Again because – alpha.

Call it mother's intuition or the need to knock Leopold's attitude down a smidgen, she'd confirmed they were having twin girls two weeks ago. It was as if the girls had been in perfect posing position during her ultrasound to prove Brianna right.

She'd been torn learning about the girls. They were healthy and strong. Her concern was the elders. How would they react to Leopold's heirs being girls rather than boys? From what she understood, there were other female leaders of prides and packs. But Leopold held *senior* leadership positions. She was terrified he'd end up being stripped of his authority as if he hadn't produced heirs at all. So, she hadn't said anything, too afraid to. But with her due date a week away, she needed to tell him.

"Leo?" Now was as good a time as any.

His ears twitched. His lion wasn't asleep.

Although filled with babies, she had an empty feeling in the pit of her stomach. "I love you." What a coward she was.

He growled/purred in response and Brianna felt his love wash over her.

"I need to tell you something."

One of the lion's eyes opened.

Before she could get the words out, she felt a pop and a sudden gush of fluid between her legs and pressure in her pelvic area. Damn it.

She took a deep breath. It would be fine. She needed to remain calm. "Leo. My water just broke."

Before her eyes, Leopold shifted back into his human form. It never ceased to amaze her. He immediately sprang into action making calls, setting their birth plan into motion.

At her insistence he'd helped her into dry panties and pants, and they were on their way to the hospital in minutes.

"It's going to be fine, mate. We'll be at the hospital in a matter of minutes. Sem will be there before we are." Leopold assured her.

Dr. Sem Jansen was a member of their pride and had been absolutely wonderful during her pregnancy. He'd vowed not to tell Leopold about the twin girls, so Brianna could. Her time had run out.

"*Leopold*, I need to tell you something about the babies." With a slow hardening grip of her abdomen, her first contraction began. It felt as if the organs in Brianna's midsection were being twisted and wrung out. She cried out in pain.

Leopold reached for her hand and squeezed gently, his face serious. "It's Leo. The babies are healthy and strong, I know that already. Hold on, we're almost there."

Tears streamed down her cheeks when another contraction hit, this time her spine feeling like it was being twisted up in knots. She practiced her breathing but it fucking hurt.

Their car screeched to a stop in front of the emergency room doors. A nurse with a wheelchair appeared to be waiting for them along with Benjamin.

"Birthing room is ready." Benjamin announced as she was placed in the wheelchair. She squeezed Leopold's and Benjamin's hands on the elevator ride to her deluxe three-room suite. It was more like an apartment than a hospital room. She'd initially thought the luxury accommodations would be too much, but now, not so much.

"Maybe I need to soak in the tub?" Brianna

suggested as her contraction ended and they wheeled her to her suite.

"We'll see what Sem says after he examines you."

With efficiency she was grateful for, she was changed into a hospital gown and lying on the soft suite mattress with her legs in stirrups. Benjamin had left the room, offering them their privacy, but not before a quick hug for his cousin, closest friend, and alpha.

Another contraction seized her, and Brianna held her breath until it passed. The girls were coming. Now.

"We're having girls." Brianna blurted out before it was too late.

Leopold gazed at her curiously. "I know. How do *you* know?"

He knew? Had Sem told him?

She and Leopold both glared at Sem. His eyes grew wide.

"You betrayed me." Brianna and Leopold accused Sem in unison.

Understanding and compassion hovered in Sem's eyes. "No. I did not betray either of you. Queen, the shifters scented you were carrying girls quite a while ago. Alpha, the queen asked for an ultrasound two weeks ago because she wanted to know the sex of your heirs. I couldn't refuse her, could I? She's my patient and I swore an oath."

Leopold and the shifters had known all this time she was carrying girls? No one had said anything? Why had Leopold insisted and bragged about his sons? Was it because he was upset? Or hoped what he'd scented was wrong?

Another contraction began and a nurse rushed in. "We can talk about it later. The girls are ready to meet their mommy and daddy. I can see one of the heads."

Sem was right. Brianna felt the intense pressure, burning and stretching associated with a baby's crowning.

"I'm scared. I don't think I can do this." She admitted. Leopold kissed her damp forehead.

"I *know* you can because you are powerful, beautiful, brilliant, and brave. You are my mate, my queen, my life." Was Leopold's heartfelt response to her doubts and fears.

Brianna had read and been told after the babies were finally delivered, with a great rush, she'd most likely feel a strong sense of relief and even euphoria. All thanks to a big release of the calming hormone oxytocin. The feline sanctuaries used an oxytocin mist on the animals for the same reason.

She hadn't truly believed it, but after a relatively quick labor, she lay back on her comfortable bed while Sem and the nurse cleaned up her and Leopold's little girls, relieved and somewhat blissful. The first weighed in at six pounds, five ounces and the second, born three minutes after her "older" sister, weighed six pounds, one ounce. A decent size for twins.

Brianna knew she only had about an hour before her idyllic state began to fade and she'd start to feel the pain and soreness from what her body had been through. She planned on enjoying every minute of her respite before that happened.

Sem brought baby number one to Leopold and placed the little pink wrapped bundle in his huge, protective arms. The nurse placed baby number two in hers. With dark blonde hair and blue eyes, just like their father, they were absolutely beautiful. Brianna felt so blessed.

After Sem and the nurse left her suite, she glanced at Leopold. His eyes beamed with happiness, and he wore a goofy grin on his handsome face. Her gaze went from one baby to the other.

"I can't tell them apart. Their slight weight difference doesn't help." Having identical twins wasn't going to be easy, she realized. Didn't twins like to play tricks on their parents when they got older? Pretending to be the other twin.

Leopold placed a featherlight kiss on the forehead of the little bundle he was holding. "They smell different. Don't worry, I'll help you tell them apart."

"You're not upset we had girls? I feel like an idiot that everyone knew except for me. The shifters. Why did you have me believing we were having boys all this time?" Brianna didn't understand her husband. She'd agonized over telling him the gender of their twins once she'd found out.

He turned his apologetic gaze on her. "I was embarrassed I was wrong, is the short answer. I'm sorry. I thought you would have realized. Sensed the lie, but you never said anything."

Brianna clenched her jaw and rocked her daughter. "I was distracted being pregnant."

Leopold had the decency to appear remorseful. "I'm sorry. It was wrong of me. I'll never lie to you again. You have my word."

Brianna needed to get back to her concern. "The elders know, then? They're not going to revoke your leadership because we had girls instead of boys?"

His posture stiffened. "They know, and I don't give a fuck what they think about it. There are plenty of female leaders among us. If for some reason they make issue with it later, they can revoke whatever they want. I have no interest in playing those games with them again. Now, on to more important things. What should we call our little princesses?"

Brianna had given their names serious thought for the last two weeks after she'd learned she was carrying girls. "I was thinking Tessa Rose for the one you're holding, the older one, after my mother, and Skylar Marie after yours for the one I'm holding."

His blue eyes sparkled with gratitude and relief washed over her. "Perfect."

Leopold had changed into black silk pajamas after Brianna had nursed the twins, who'd taken to nursing like the champions he knew they'd be. He'd be spending the night until his ladies were discharged in the next couple of days.

He and his mate had been treated to a personal chef prepared filet mignon dinner after the girls had been placed in their shared hospital crib. He'd snapped photos of them after they'd reached out to each other and clasped hands before falling asleep. They were beyond precious.

And although the custom blankets he'd had made for them were too large for them now, one hung over the end of the crib. The embroidery read – *Raise a daughter that people are a little bit afraid of. Teach her to be fierce and independent, and to not care what people think. Raise her to be a warrior who is going to change the world and make a difference.*

He and Brianna would teach and guide Tessa Rose and Skylar Marie. The twins were the future of his pride and those under his leadership. Future businesswomen. Warriors in training.

Leopold couldn't have imagined nearly a year and a half ago, that he'd be where he was now. Mated and married to the most amazing woman he hadn't realized existed or had even considered needing, a new father to beautiful twin girls who would one day follow in his footsteps, and his personal and family business interests grew more successful every day.

His lion whined to be set free and nuzzle the babies, but Leopold couldn't risk being discovered by the human hospital staff. His lion would have to wait until they were all safely at home.

Brianna soaked in the jacuzzi tub tucked in the corner of the suite's bedroom with her eyes closed and a smile on her face. The pain of childbirth had finally caught up with her. She'd needed the rest and relief.

"How are you doing over there? Ready to get out yet?" Leopold wanted to get them tucked into bed so she could get some much needed and well-earned sleep.

"I think so, yes. The water's cooling. Do you mind helping me?" Brianna asked, her smile not faltering.

"Of course not." He'd do anything for his woman, didn't she realize that yet?

Leopold helped his wife out of the tub and wrapped her in a fluffy towel. He brushed his lips against hers and kissed Brianna slow and sweet. He'd never conceived of loving anyone as much as he loved his mate. Then his babies were born, and he'd discovered he had an infinite capacity to love.

He helped her dress and get into bed without too much discomfort. He glanced at the crib beside their bed. He'd hoped they could all sleep together, but the girls were sleeping soundly. Leopold didn't want to risk waking them. Brianna needed her sleep as well.

Leopold slipped into bed and gently gathered Brianna against him. She snuggled close and sighed. The scent of her favorite lily-scented bubble bath lingered on her skin. That mixed with her natural, tantalizing scent soothed his soul.

"I can't believe we have two beautiful little babies. Are you ready for what comes next?"

Brianna yawned and her eyes drifted closed. He felt her relax and surrender to her exhaustion.

They were incredibly blessed. Leopold *was* ready for what came next, and he couldn't think of anyone he'd rather have beside him for the journey that lay ahead.

The End

Bonus Content – Leopold's Love Notes

I wanted to share **all** of the love note ideas I had to choose from for the story. There were so many that couldn't be included in the story itself, but I wanted to make them available to all of you.

You can use them for yourself - tuck them in your partner's pants pocket, briefcase or purse, send a sweet text message, include a love note in their lunch, etc. Be creative. And naughty too!

- You make my soul smile.
- I love you. You are the rest of my life.
- You are powerful, beautiful, brilliant, and brave. You are my mate, my queen, my life.

- It's not just what I feel for you; it's what I don't want to feel for anyone else.
- Love doesn't need to be perfect. It just needs to be real. True.
- I stand behind you, because I trust you to lead the way. I lead the way because I know you always have my back.
- When we have each other, we have everything.
- A real king knows how to take care of his queen.
- How can you give me so much strength and yet still be my only weakness?
- You're not rich until you have something money can't buy.
- A lion never roars after a kill.
- You are like water, keeping me alive, keeping me afloat, and thirsting for you.
- Let me kiss you now, so I can taste the flavors of your sweetness.
- It's not how big the house is, it's how happy the home is.
- You grab me by my heartstrings and play your love's music.
- You are my divine, not my sin.

- I never knew mates/love had a flavor until I tasted the sweetness of your lips on my tongue.
- Sometimes all I need is for you to hold and heal me.
- Time stands still when I'm with you.
- Tell me where you want my lips to go and get lost on their journey there.
- You're the only one who can hear everything I've never said.
- You can excite me by doing nothing at all, just by being you.
- Vulnerability is sexy. I will unzip my heart and share it with you.
- I love you the only way I know how. Completely.
- Your voice and laughter were my favorite sounds until I heard you moan.
- I wanted to be valued. Heard. Seen.
- There is a place in my heart that has been waiting for you.
- I hear you the loudest when you haven't said a thing.
- Take me inside your wildest dreams, inside your wildest heart.
- I will keep your heart safe, tucked inside my soul.

- If love is blind, I'll use my soul to see you and my heart to feel you.
- I feel the things you don't say.
- The only way I will ever leave you, is breathless.
- All I need are your hands on my skin and your fingers in my hair.
- I will help you stand tall, and leave your legs shaking.
- The only thing I want, is to be wanted by you.
- Let my soul touch you in ways my body cannot.
- I've been yours since the moment we met.
- Your kisses take my breath away and leave me feeling dizzy and drunk.
- The feel of your skin against mine is more addictive than any drug.
- Tell me mate, whose ass is this? Whose tits are these? Whose body is this?
- Your heart, future, life are safe in my hands.
- The amount of fucking I want to do right now is ridiculous.
- My love for you will never die.

About the Author

Int'l bestseller and award-winning author **Dania Voss** writes compelling, sexy romance with personality, heat, and heart. Born in Rome, Italy and raised in Chicagoland, she creates stories with authentic, engaging characters. She loves anything pink and is a huge fan of 80s hair bands.

A favorite with romance readers, her debut novel "On the Ropes," the first in her Windy City Nights series, became an international bestseller. Dania's books have won multiple awards, and her work has been highlighted on NBC, ABC, CBS, and FOX. She has been featured in the Chicago Tribune, Southern Writers Magazine, and Chicago Entrepreneurs Magazine (selected as the #8 Top Chicago Author in 2021). The Windy City Nights series (in digital format) is going to the moon in 2023, as part of the Writers on the Moon project.

When she's not writing, you can find Dania at a sporting event, a rock concert, or the movies (preferably a comedy).

Also by Dania Voss

Read More from Dania Voss

https://books.bookfunnel.com/authordaniavoss

Newsletter

https://dl.bookfunnel.com/ach2oysc7o

Website

https://www.daniavoss.com